SHATTERED

SHATTERED

ERIC WALTERS

WITH A FOREWORD BY ROMÉO DALLAIRE

VIKING
CANADA

VIKING CANADA

Published by the Penguin Group

Penguin Group (Canada), 90 Eglinton Avenue East, Suite 700, Toronto, Ontario, Canada M4P 2Y3
(a division of Pearson Penguin Canada Inc.)

Penguin Group (USA) Inc., 375 Hudson Street, New York, New York 10014, U.S.A.
Penguin Books Ltd, 80 Strand, London WC2R 0RL, England
Penguin Ireland, 25 St Stephen's Green, Dublin 2, Ireland (a division of Penguin Books Ltd)
Penguin Group (Australia), 250 Camberwell Road, Camberwell, Victoria 3124, Australia
(a division of Pearson Australia Group Pty Ltd)
Penguin Books India Pvt Ltd, 11 Community Centre, Panchsheel Park, New Delhi – 110 017, India
Penguin Group (NZ), cnr Airborne and Rosedale Roads, Albany, Auckland 1310, New Zealand
(a division of Pearson New Zealand Ltd)
Penguin Books (South Africa) (Pty) Ltd, 24 Sturdee Avenue, Rosebank, Johannesburg 2196, South Africa

Penguin Books Ltd, Registered Offices: 80 Strand, London WC2R 0RL, England

First published 2006

1 2 3 4 5 6 7 8 9 10   (FR)

Copyright © Eric Walters, 2006
Foreword copyright © Roméo Dallaire
Map of Rwanda copyright © Paul Sneath, free&Creative
Interior illustrations copyright © Johann Wessels

Author representation: Westwood Creative Artists
94 Harbord Street, Toronto, Ontario M5S 1G6

*Publisher's note: This book is a work of fiction. Names, characters, places and incidents either
are the product of the author's imagination or are used fictitiously, and any resemblance
to actual persons living or dead, events, or locales is entirely coincidental.*

A percentage of the author's royalties will be donated to charities of benefit to children in Rwanda.

Manufactured in Canada.

LIBRARY AND ARCHIVES CANADA CATALOGUING IN PUBLICATION

Walters, Eric, 1957–

Shattered / Eric Walters.

ISBN-13: 978-0-670-06366-6
ISBN-10: 0-670-06366-5

I. Title.

PS8595.A598S53   2006   jC813'.54   C2005-905629-0

Visit the Penguin Group (Canada) website at **www.penguin.ca**

One death is a tragedy; a million is a statistic.

—JOSEPH STALIN

All that is required for evil to prevail is for good men to do nothing.

—EDMUND BURKE

Foreword

I SERVED IN THE CANADIAN MILITARY, as did my father before me. My father was a role model for me, perhaps a bit more stern than I would have liked, but nevertheless a man of high moral standards and example. Much of my success in life is due in no small measure to the values and principles he was able to instill in me. He was my mentor in "ways military," explaining the code of military discipline and the conduct of a non-commissioned officer.

The story you are about to read is not about me, although there are similarities, but it is about a fictional soldier who has been through some of my experiences and many more. He represents a new type of veteran, released from his military family because he can no longer perform his military duties as a result of an injury sustained in operations. Had he suffered a physical injury, he would be accepted in society as an honourable veteran wounded in a foreign war, but this fellow has no visible injuries, so he is seen, as so many others like him, as just another failed soldier, gotten rid of because he is now damaged goods.

It is a case that unfortunately is far too close to reality. The author has captured the frustration of the injured soldier and society's indifference to both him and the street people with whom he lives. In our rush to material success and its rewards, we are prone to stereotype people without pausing to consider the circumstances of the less fortunate and how we can help those who have become marginalized to find some semblance of a tolerable if not a rewarding life.

The worse offence is to fail to recognize these injured people as fellow humans in our wonderfully affluent society. To belittle their condition is unpardonable. We will be looked upon by history by the way we treated our wounded and downtrodden.

In this story, the reader will encounter characters who, over time, discover their own compassion toward those who are wounded. They may well be the heroes of our time.

Roméo Dallaire
Ottawa, October 2005

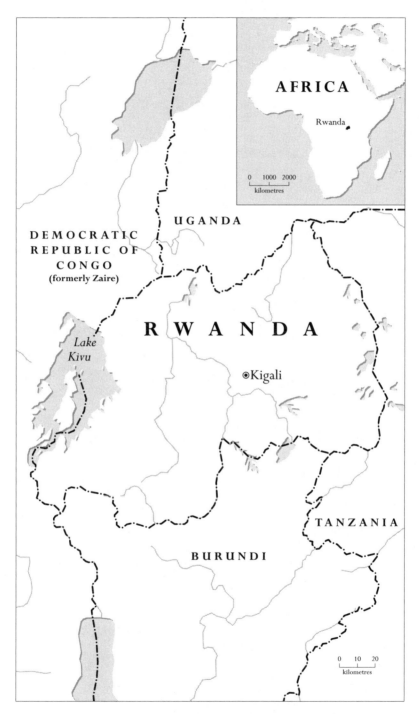

Map of Rwanda

One

I TURNED THE COLLAR UP on my ski jacket. The wind was bitterly cold and was blowing directly into my face. It was the first day of spring but it didn't feel like it. Instead it was just another cold day in an endless winter of cold, snowy days. At least it wasn't snowing right now. It was the coldest winter I could remember. My father told me there was one even worse twelve years ago but I was only three then and couldn't remember that far back.

I looked at my watch. It was almost ten to six. I had just over ten minutes to get there. It wasn't good to be late for a job interview. Then again, it was an interview for a *volunteer* job. What was the worst that could happen? That I wouldn't get a job that didn't *pay* that I didn't *want* to do to begin with?

Then I thought about what would happen if I didn't get the job. My civics teacher had made it clear that if I didn't get this job she wasn't arranging another interview for me. And she'd made it equally clear that if I didn't get a placement, I couldn't pass, and my father had already told me what would happen then. If I didn't get all of my credits there wasn't going to be any car for a birthday present.

My father had promised me a car when I turned sixteen. That was what his father had done for him and what he'd said he was going to do for me. I didn't know what type, but he'd been hinting around about a BMW. It probably wouldn't be anything fancy—maybe something in the 300 series. My father could afford to buy me a Beamer. He could afford to buy a *dozen* Beamers. Maybe he wasn't around that much but the money helped make up for that. Now, thinking about the car, the job interview had some real meaning. I doubled my pace.

As I walked I kept my head up, looking around. I didn't know the downtown very well at all. The times I'd come here were with my parents for hockey games, shows, or shopping and this certainly wasn't the part we'd been to. There were no theatres or fancy stores anywhere to be seen.

Instead the buildings were run-down and seemed to be limited to dollar stores, pawn shops, laundromats, and cheque cashing stores. A couple of the stores had boards over the glass, the boards plastered with posters and advertisements. Some of them even had curtains in the windows—failed retail had become street-level apartments.

The streets themselves were dirty and strewn with garbage. It was dreary and depressing. But that shouldn't have been any surprise to me. Where else would they put a soup kitchen to feed street people?

I shook my head. I still couldn't believe this. I was going to be doing my community hours at a soup kitchen. That sounded like something out of bad movie or a book by John Steinbeck. But I didn't have anybody to blame but myself. Why had I been so stupid? I hadn't bothered to read the information in the booklet listing all the volunteer jobs. I just saw the name of the program—"The Club." I thought it sounded classy. I guess it did have class ... the lowest class possible. Then when my teacher told me what it really was, I couldn't back out. She'd already been on my case about how I was always taking the easiest route, how I always cut corners on assignments, and that I didn't take her class seriously. She was right. I didn't take her class— or any class—seriously. She then went on to tell me how *surprised* she was by my choice and that maybe she'd *misjudged* me. The truth was that she hadn't misjudged me.

She actually made me a little uneasy. I got the feeling that she was always trying to figure everybody out. I hated people like that. Especially those people who actually *did* have you figured out.

I just wished I'd been smart enough to start my placement—any placement—when everybody else had started theirs. Somehow I'd just hoped that I could skate by without doing it. And when she didn't mention it to me, week after week, I thought that somehow she'd forgotten about it too. Now I only had three months to finish up what had taken other people six or seven months to do.

So here I was, heading to the Club. Obviously somebody's idea of a joke. Unfortunately the joke was now on me.

The time was tight. It was still one block down and one block over. There was a park on my right side. If I went through the park I could cut the angle and maybe I could just make it. I turned onto the gravel path that led diagonally across the park—exactly the direction I needed to go.

I'd travelled no more than a dozen steps when I had second thoughts. This wasn't the best neighbourhood and it was starting to get dark. I looked around anxiously. I didn't see anybody. I guess even bums had better places to be than hanging around a park in the cold and dark. I'd keep my head up and my eyes open and—

"You got a smoke to spare?"

I jumped into the air, spun around, and stifled the urge to scream. There was a man standing in the shadows, just off from the path. I'd walked right by him and hadn't seen him at all. So much for keeping my eyes open.

The man stepped out of the shadows and into the open. My heart was still pounding but I took a good look at him. He was dressed in a large, dirty, green parka. He had a matching green toque pulled low on his head, a few days' growth of greying, gritty beard on his face.

"I didn't mean to scare you," he said apologetically. He sounded like he meant it.

"You didn't scare me … I was just … just startled … that's all," I stammered.

"Didn't mean to do that either. You got an extra smoke I can have?"

"I don't smoke."

"Smart. Wish I didn't either. Any spare change?" he asked.

"Sure." I unzipped my jacket and reached inside, pulling my wallet out of the pocket. I opened it up and—

"Put that away!" he snapped.

I looked up at him confused and a little scared. What was he talking about, what did he mean?

"Put that wallet back in your pocket," he ordered.

"But I was just trying to give you some change," I tried to explain.

"I understand that—I appreciate that—but you can't be waving a wallet around here. You never know who's watching." He looked stern and serious.

Slowly I looked around. There were trees and bushes casting long shadows, but the park was deserted except for him and me. "I don't see anybody."

"Just because you can't see *them,* doesn't mean they can't see *you.*" He paused. "Just put it away."

I stuffed my wallet back into my pocket.

"You just have to be careful," he said. "You never know who's around."

I nodded my head. Did he really think we were being watched or was he just crazy? I'd heard about people like this—what was the word—paranoid, that was it, paranoid. I knew that a lot of the people who lived on the street were mentally ill—psychiatric patients—and that they heard voices in their heads, or saw things that weren't there or believed people were watching them, were out to get them. But this guy didn't seem crazy. Then again, how did I know what was going on inside his brain? If he really was normal, would he be out here begging for change?

"There are people who would split your head open for a couple of bucks and you have more than a couple of bucks—I saw the bills when you opened your wallet."

I stepped back a half step.

"It's not me you have to worry about," he continued. "There's not enough money in any wallet to make me hurt another human being."

I didn't know him—he was just some street person begging smokes and change—but somehow I believed him.

"I think I have some change in my pocket ... not much, but some," I said.

"Anything you have would be appreciated," he said softly, looking down at the ground.

I dug into my pocket and rummaged around. There were a few coins jingling together. I pulled them out and looked. There wasn't much—a quarter, a couple of dimes, and three or four pennies. I dropped them into his outstretched hand.

"Thank you," he said.

"You're welcome. I'm sorry there isn't more."

"I appreciate what you gave. Some people, they don't even turn their heads—they act like you're not there." He paused. "It's getting dark," he said. "You shouldn't be here when it's dark."

"I'm just cutting through. I have an interview in—" I looked down at my watch. "Right now. I got to get going." I rushed off down the path.

"Thanks!" he yelled and I looked over my shoulder. He gave a little wave. "Be careful!" he called out. I nodded and kept going.

Strange. Not what I'd expected. A bum who was polite—and well spoken. He had a trace of some sort of accent ... I couldn't tell what, but something. There was also something else about him. Maybe it was the manners—I hadn't expected that—or the way he stood. His shoulders were back, his posture perfect. Strange.

With his warning to be careful, I tried to be more aware of what was around me. Coming up to a bench beside the path, I realized that it was occupied. There was a man stretched out on it. He was covered by a tattered old blanket pulled over top of him so only his head was peeking out. I shifted slightly over to the other side of the path as I passed by. What a place to sleep. The guy had to be crazy, or drunk, or both.

Up ahead, coming directly toward me along the path, was a woman pushing a shopping cart. The wheels were digging into the gravel and she was struggling to keep it moving. She was all stooped over and had a pronounced limp. Her clothing was a crazy patchwork quilt of colours and materials and items. The cart was piled high and as she got closer I could see that it wasn't filled with groceries. There were empty bottles, folded cardboard boxes, newspapers, and clothing—rags. She was pushing a cart filled with garbage.

As she got even closer I heard her talking to herself. It was a loud, profane rant about the government. I squeezed over to the very edge of the path to create as much distance between us as possible. As she got close her monologue got louder and louder.

She looked up at me. "Cold one, ain't it," she said, and flashed me a smile.

"Yeah, cold," I mumbled. Crazy but friendly.

I looked back over my shoulder and watched—and listened—as she continued both her journey and her rant. I couldn't help but wonder what was going on in her head. What demons were driving her? But I didn't have time to even think about that. I had to get going as fast as I—

"Hey!"

I jerked my head to the side. Two men—really, older teenagers—were cutting across the grass toward me. I turned away and kept walking. Maybe they weren't even talking to—

"Wait up, kid!"

There was no doubt now. Should I stop or run or— Another man appeared on the path directly in front of me.

"He told you to wait," the third man said.

A shiver went up my spine as I skidded to a stop directly in front of him. He stood there in the middle of the path, blocking my way. The path was narrow at this point, boxed in by hedges on both sides. It was sheltered … and isolated. I looked past him, up the path. There was nobody in sight.

I turned around. The other two were closing in and there was nobody else in sight in that direction either. Even the shopping cart lady had disappeared around the corner. Quickly they closed the space until they were right behind me and I was caught in the middle, trapped. I felt a wave of panic sweep over me. What did they want? Had they seen me pull out my wallet? Were these the people that guy had warned me about, the people who were watching?

They were all dressed in black, leather jackets, thick-soled boots. They looked like thugs, not people living on the street. I felt scared—no, worse than scared. I almost felt sick.

"Nice shoes," one of them said. He was clearly the biggest of the three—not just taller but thicker, more muscular. The other two weren't much bigger than me.

"Um … thanks," I mumbled. They were practically new, top-of-the-line Air Jordans. They were a Christmas present from my grandmother.

"What size are they?" asked one of the two guys who had caught up to me from behind.

"What size?" I repeated.

"You don't hear so good, do you?" said the one standing in front—the biggest of the three. "What friggin' size are they?" He spoke low and slow and there was an ominous quality to his words. This wasn't somebody I wanted to screw around with.

"Size eleven." Why did he want to know what size? I suddenly got a terrible feeling I knew why he was asking.

"Size eleven. This is my lucky day. That's *my* size. Take 'em off."

"You're joking, right?"

He stepped forward and with lightning speed reaching out, grabbed me by the jacket and practically lifted me off my feet. "Do I look like I'm the sorta guy who jokes around?" he demanded angrily.

"But they're my shoes," I said, trying to sound defiant.

"They were your shoes," he said as he tightened his grip on my shirt.

My feeble attempt at defiance dissolved. "But ... but ... I need my shoes," I stammered.

"As much as you need your life?" he asked. "Take off your shoes!"

I wanted to run, I wanted to fight, I wanted to say something back, to argue. There was no way or no point in any of those. Instead I pleaded.

"But, you can't just leave me standing in my socks."

"You got a choice. Either we leave you *standing* here or *lying* here. You take 'em off or we do it for you." He pulled me even closer, so close that we were practically nose to nose, so close that his stinking, foul breath was all I could breathe. "Me, I don't care which way it happens ... might be a little bonus to bust your head first."

"I'll take them off," I mumbled, trying to look away. There was no point in fighting. If there'd been just one of them, maybe I could have put up a fight, but all three? There was no way. Big deal, so they got my shoes. I had a dozen other pairs at home and could replace these easily.

"Smart." He released his grip.

I hesitated for a second. This was like some sort of bad dream. This wasn't—I stumbled forward as I was shoved from behind and jolted back to reality.

"Hurry up!" one of the guys behind me ordered.

I bent down and undid the laces on the first shoe, pulling my foot free. It felt cold and exposed. I put it down on the gravel and the cold and wet radiated up my foot and into my leg. I looked past them, hoping somebody, anybody, would be there on the path coming toward us—there was nobody.

"Give it here!" he yelled as he jerked the shoe from my hand. "Now the other one."

I used my sock foot to push off the second shoe. I bent down, grabbed it, and handed it to the guy holding the first shoe. He held them up over his head, like he was showing off some prize that he won. He started to chuckle and I felt like an even bigger fool.

"You got any money?" he asked.

"Nothing, I don't have anything," I lied, shaking my head.

"You lyin'? I don't like liars. You lie to me and we'll be layin' a beatin' on you."

"I'm not lying ... honest ... I gave away what I had to one of the panhandlers," I explained. My mouth was dry and I could feel my hands trembling, but I still wasn't going to hand over my money to these jerks.

"How nice. You gave some bum your cash and us your shoes. What a nice guy you are," he taunted and the other two began laughing.

"Don't worry about it, man," one of the two behind me said, "the night is still young. We might get that money anyway ... if we roll the right bum."

They all started laughing, but there was no joy or happiness in the laughter. It was mean, evil. They weren't just after my shoes or my money. They were enjoying this.

"Now, let's have your coat," the big guy, who was obviously the leader, said.

"Come on, not my coat … please." It wasn't just my coat. It was my wallet in the inside pocket with all of my ID and money. What would they do when they found out I'd lied to them and really did have money?

"Give us your coat!"

"I think he probably wants to keep his coat," came a voice from behind. We all spun around. It was him—the man I'd given the change to.

"If you got half a brain you'd stay out of this," snarled the leader.

"Leave the kid alone," the man said, sounding very calm.

"This ain't your business, you old rubby. Just go away and find yourself some aftershave to drink."

"I'm not leaving without my friend here."

"You stupid or drunk or both?" demanded the guy holding my shoes.

"Just leave the kid alone. He hasn't done anything wrong."

"We'll leave him alone after we get his coat!" the biggest of the three snarled.

"Do you want my coat instead?" the man asked. "You can have it if you want."

"Yours? You think I want to wear something you've worn? Probably filled with lice."

"I don't know about lice, but what about this?" He pulled a long piece of metal out of his sleeve. It was half as long as his arm and as thick as a thumb. The man held the metal rod up, turning it around, like he was examining it for the first time, like he had never seen it before. As it turned, the rod caught some of the fading rays of the sun and glistened.

"Pretty nice, eh?" he asked.

The two guys between us backed away until all three of them stood side by side. I staggered forward so that the man was now between them and me.

"You really think you're scaring us?" the leader asked.

"Not trying to scare anybody. Just want us to walk away in one direction and the three of you go in the other."

"You're not goin' anywhere except down ... let's take 'em!" the guy yelled.

The three thugs surged forward. Lightning-like, the man jumped to the side and with his leg swept the feet out from under the leader, who crashed to the gravel with a heavy thud! Almost in the same motion he brought the metal rod down on the leg of a second, who screamed out in pain as he collapsed to a heap on the ground. The third one skidded to a stop. The man stepped toward him, swinging the metal rod in the air, and the young guy turned and ran away. Now the man spun around and leaped forward until he was standing over top of the two thugs.

"Don't move!" he yelled.

I stood stock still before I realized he wasn't talking to me.

One of the two tried to get back up. The man reached over and kicked his arm out from under him and he crashed back down to the ground. The other one was clutching his leg, rolling around in pain.

"Shoes," the man said, pointing the metal rod at them.

"Sure ... he can have them ... we weren't really goin' to take them," the leader whimpered. He didn't sound so brave now—or look so big. He reached to the ground where my shoes had fallen when he was knocked down. He held them out for me.

Cautiously I inched forward and took them. "Thanks," I said. That sounded stupid.

"Now your shoes," the man said.

"What?" the thug asked.

"I want *all* the shoes. *Your* shoes … and his," he said, pointing at them with the metal bar.

"But—"

"Now!" He took the bar and slammed it against one of the shrubs, causing the wood to splinter.

Both thugs scrambled to undo their laces.

"No, wait!" he ordered. "You get to keep your shoes," he said, pointing to the guy whose leg he'd hurt. He pointed to the other. "I want your shoes *and* your coat … I hope it doesn't have lice."

The thug looked shocked and then angry and then like he was going to say something, but he didn't. Instead he took off his second shoe and then slipped out of his jacket.

"Get up."

The injured one had trouble rising—he was barely able to put weight on the one leg. He was grimacing in pain and his face was stained with tears.

"Now get out of this park and I don't ever want to see either of you back here again."

"This isn't the end," the big guy said. Suddenly, on his feet, he was feeling more confident again.

"It is the end unless you want to lose your *pants* as well."

I almost laughed but restrained myself. The thug now seemed more comical than threatening as he stood there without his leather jacket, bouncing around on his stocking feet—his big toe sticking out of a hole in the one sock.

"I won't forget you or what happened," the thug said. Brave words, but I noticed he kept his distance.

"I don't want you to forget," the bum said. "I want you to remember … remember what happens if you pick on people." His voice was calm, quiet, but menacing. "Remember, if you come back here again, it won't just be your shoes and jacket that you lose." He held the rod up. "You have any idea what would have happened if I'd hit him in the head instead of the leg?"

Neither of them answered.

"You want to find out?" the man demanded as he stepped toward them, waving the rod in the air.

The two men hurried away.

"Come on back!" he yelled, but they kept moving, not looking back.

We stood there and watched as they limped off into the gathering darkness, the one with his arm around the other, helping him move. The sun was almost completely down and it was becoming darker by the second.

"Are you all right?" the bum asked.

"I'm okay ... a little shaky ... but okay ... thanks." In truth I felt scared and confused and upset.

"Put on your shoes."

I bent down and slipped on the first shoe, untied the second, and put it on. My feet were cold and my socks wet. I quickly tied my laces up.

"What are you going to do with those?" I asked, pointing to the leather jacket and pair of boots lying on the ground beside me.

"I almost forgot." He picked up the jacket and tossed it into a garbage can. Next he grabbed one of the boots. "These are the sort of boots a soldier wears." He shook his head in disgust. "What an insult to soldiers ... men prepared to sacrifice their lives to protect our country and save others' lives ... even the lives of scum like those three. Come, I'll walk you out of the park."

I was going to say that wasn't necessary, but it was—I didn't want to walk alone, not now, after all that had happened, and certainly not in the dark. We walked along in silence. I wanted to say something to him. I didn't know exactly how to say it, but I had to try.

"It was lucky for me that you came along when you did," I said.

"Luck had nothing to do with it. This is not the best place to be, so I figured maybe it would be good for me to stay close, until you got out of the park."

"I didn't see you following me."

He laughed. "You weren't *supposed* to see me. I was off to the side, staying among the trees and bushes and shadows. If nothing happened you wouldn't have known I was ever there."

"But you thought something would happen."

"I thought something *could* happen," he answered. "I told you this place isn't safe … especially not at night. It's good to have at least one friend with you—that's why I always carry this," he said, holding up the metal rod.

"I'm pretty happy you had that with you."

He shrugged. "Most people who live out here have something to protect themselves."

"People carry around pieces of metal?"

"Pieces of metal, pipes, box cutters, knives, machetes."

"People have machetes?" I questioned. I found that hard to believe.

He nodded. "They can be pretty deadly."

"I can't even imagine what it would do to somebody if you hit them with a machete."

"I don't have to imagine," he said, his words so quiet that I almost didn't hear him.

His answer startled me. Did that mean he didn't have to imagine because he'd seen it happen or because he'd done it himself? I edged slightly away from him. He'd saved me, but I didn't know anything about him other than he was some bum, a bum who carried a metal rod up his sleeve, a metal rod that he'd just used to smash some guy in the leg, maybe breaking it for all I knew. And worse still, he'd basically threatened to kill them if they came back ... *kill* them. What was to stop him from hitting *me* in the side of the head with it if I said something he didn't like, or if some crazy voice in his head told him to?

Up ahead I could see the street lights, and then flashes of cars passing by, and then finally the street itself. I felt a huge sense of relief. I'd be awfully happy to get out of that park and back onto the sidewalk. We stopped when we came to the street.

"You okay from here?" he asked.

"Sure, no problem. I really appreciate what you did. I don't know what would have happened if you hadn't come along."

"I have a pretty good idea," he said.

That sent a shudder up my spine. I had a pretty good idea too. "Thanks again for what you did."

"You want to really thank me?" he asked.

"Sure." I started to reach for my wallet.

"Don't pull that out," he snapped. "I don't want any more of your money. You already gave me some change."

"But I have more I could give to let you know how much I appreciate what—"

"The best thing you could give me—the way to thank me—is to *never* come to this park at night again. Okay?"

"You don't have to worry about that."

"Good. You'll be fine. Stay on the street. Do you have far to go now?"

"It's just up ahead."

"You better get going. The street is safer than the park, but that doesn't make it safe. Keep your eyes open and your head up, understand?"

I nodded. I wasn't going to let anybody sneak up on me again. I started off. I got partway down the block and then stopped and turned around. He was still standing there, watching—watching over me. I waved and he waved back. He turned and headed into the park. He quickly vanished into the darkness. Maybe he was just a bum. Maybe he was even crazy. But he'd been my guardian angel and he was gone. I suddenly felt open and exposed. I looked all around. I wondered if I was being watched. I hurried up the street.

Two

THERE WERE VERY FEW PEOPLE on the street, so I was surprised when I saw a line of people pressed against a building up ahead. I was just about to reach into my pocket and pull out the slip of paper that had the address written on it when it suddenly connected in my head—this was probably the place. As I got closer I saw a sign on the building—THE CLUB. The lettering was in bright orange paint, crudely done and peeling away.

The men in line, and I noticed that it *was* all men, were huddled together, like they were shielding each other from the wind and the cold. They stood unmoving, as still and silent as statues. As I walked by I became aware that not a single person reacted to my passing. Nobody said anything or even looked over. Their eyes were locked on the ground, staring at their feet. Nobody was making any eye contact with anybody else.

With them not looking at me I felt free to look at them. They were dressed in a shoddy assortment of coats and hats and scarves and boots and shoes. Nothing seemed to match anything else. It was obvious that some men had on layers and layers of clothing—they looked puffy. A couple weren't really even that badly dressed while some others looked as if they were clothed completely in rags, held together in defiance of gravity and sanity.

I stopped in front of a door that marked the start of the line. Should I wait or just go inside? I thought about it for a second. There was no way I was waiting out here with these people. Slowly, hesitantly, I walked to the door and gave it a little push. It opened and I peeked inside. The room was dominated by eight or ten long, long wooden tables, each flanked by benches. There wasn't a soul in sight. I edged in through the door. It was warm and there was the distinct smell of cooking. I wasn't sure what it was, but it didn't smell half bad.

A man wearing an apron and carrying a big pot came into the room through a swinging door down at the far end of the hall.

"Excuse me," I called out.

"It's almost ready, just wait outside and——" He looked up and saw me.

"I'm not here to eat," I explained. "I'm here to see Mr. MacDonald."

"I'm MacDonald."

I walked over toward him. "I'm Ian Blackburn." I held out my hand to shake. He just stared at me, looking me up and down. I suddenly felt even more nervous and unsure of myself.

He turned away and put the pot down on a counter alongside another big pot. Both were steaming hot—that's where the smell was coming from.

"So why are you here?" he asked, sounding suspicious.

I lowered my hand. "I'm here to apply for a position."

He laughed. It was a thick, heavy, throaty laugh that forced its way out. "The only position we have is upright. Standing right here behind the counter shovelling out food."

"That's what I'm here for, to be interviewed to do that ... as a volunteer."

"Volunteers we have, interviews we don't. You showed up so you get to work."

I felt relieved. Being late hadn't cost me the job. He reached down and grabbed something off the counter and tossed it to me. I unravelled it to reveal a balled-up apron. It was greyish and stained.

"Put it on and then slip on some gloves."

I started to take my coat off.

"Better leave that on. I ain't got time to lock it up in back and if you lay it down somebody might steal it … best not to lay anything down around here you don't want to walk. Some people might try to rip you off for a nice coat like that."

It wasn't much of a stretch for me to believe him. For a split second I thought of telling him what had happened and then stopped myself. I just felt embarrassed and stupid about the whole thing. I should have seen it coming.

I took a better look at him. He was a strange-looking old bird. He was shorter than me, but stocky, and looked like he could take care of himself. Actually, judging from the way his nose was all bent out of shape I was certain he'd been in more than a few fights in his time. I tried to figure out his age. His hair was grey and thin and his face was lined and weather-beaten. He had to be in his sixties, if not older.

I slipped the apron on over my head, looped the strings around my waist and tied them up.

"What did you say your name was again?" he asked.

"Ian."

"Well, Ian, I'll explain what you have to do. It isn't particularly complicated. Each man grabs one of those," he said, pointing to a pile of brown trays. "He puts a bowl and a plate and a plastic cup on it and then moves over here where you give him two scoops of food in the bowl, one slice of bread, and then I pour 'em a drink. Think you can handle that?"

"I think so."

"Some of the guys might ask you to give 'em more. Just tell 'em that they only get one serving. After everybody has eaten, if there's any left, then they can come back for seconds. Most of the fellas are regulars and know the rules, but some of 'em like to test anybody new."

"Okay, no problem, Mr. MacDonald."

"Call me Mac."

"Sure ... Mac."

"So is this just a one-night thing or are you supposed to be here for a while?" he asked.

"Forty hours."

"Is this like a court-ordered thing?" Mac asked.

"Court-ordered ... what do you mean?"

"You got convicted of something and were sentenced to do this instead of going to jail or paying a fine."

"No!" I exclaimed. "It's for school!" Did he think I looked like some sort of criminal?

"What sort of school?"

As he was talking he was wiping the counter and stirring the pot.

"My civics class. We have to do volunteer work to pass," I explained.

"So you *have* to be here."

"If I want to pass civics."

"This really isn't something you *want* to do," he said.

"Um ... I guess not," I answered reluctantly, thinking that maybe I shouldn't have admitted that.

"You're not hoping to grow up to be a social worker or something like that, are you?" he asked. He sounded suspicious.

I laughed. "That's just about the *last* thing in the world I'd want to become." The truth was, there actually had been a time I'd toyed with that idea. Then my father told me how difficult the job was and how badly it paid.

"Even better! Some of these do-gooders who come around here to do volunteer work think they're here to save souls or do therapy instead of serving food." He paused and stared at me. "You're not here to judge 'em or save 'em, just serve 'em food."

"I'm not trying to save anybody except myself … from a failing mark," I said. "I'm just trying to do my hours so I can pass."

"Good. This ain't no social project. Understand?" He wiped his hands on a discoloured dishtowel tucked into his belt.

"You don't have to worry about me. I'm going to keep my mouth shut, serve food, do my hours, and leave."

He laughed again. "Sounds like you have a lot in common with the people here."

"What do you mean?" I asked.

"None of them want to be here either. And you're smart to keep your mouth closed. Worst thing you could do is ask a lot of questions. That sometimes leads to people getting upset."

"I'm not here to ask anybody anything," I said. "I won't even talk to anybody if you don't want me to."

"Talking is fine. Just don't be giving anybody any crap."

"I don't give crap." Unless somebody tries to give it to me first, I thought but didn't say.

"Just be polite and respectful. Don't go asking a whole lot of questions. Something you think might be innocent, just sort of making conversation—like where do you live—might set somebody off … especially somebody who's paranoid. And almost everybody who walks through those doors is at least a little paranoid."

"Everybody?" I asked.

"You have to be at least a little paranoid if you want to survive living on the streets. There really are people out there who want to rip you off or hurt you. That's the way of the streets. Just remember, just 'cause somebody's paranoid doesn't mean they're not out to get him."

He chuckled to himself. "I think it's time to let them in."

I watched as he walked over to the door and opened it up.

"Come on in, boys, supper's waiting!" he called out.

The first two men shuffled in and the line snaked in behind them. Mac stood by the door, welcoming people, shaking hands, patting people on the back. He gave one old man—all bent over and dressed in absolutely filthy clothes—a hug. I shuddered, wondering what sort of diseases and bugs the old man was carrying. My scalp got all itchy just thinking about it. As soon as I got home I was going to take one very long, very hot shower.

The first man stood in front of me, tray in hand. He was wearing a big bulky parka, a thick sweater, and a scarf wrapped around his neck, the standard toque on his head. He didn't look very old, maybe in his late twenties. Across the counter and through the steam and food smell rising from the pots I could still make out the distinct odour of alcohol coming off him.

"What are you serving?" he asked.

"Um ..." I didn't know. I lifted up the lid and peered in through the rising steam. "It looks like some sort of stew." I stirred it around with the big ladle and lifted a scoop. "Beef stew."

"Mac makes great stew. Ever try it?"

"No!" I exclaimed. Did he really think that I was going to eat food from a soup kitchen? "It's my first time here," I said, trying to cover up my feelings of disgust.

"If there's any left at the end, you should try it," he said.

"If there's any left, I will," I said, although I was just saying that to humour him.

I picked up the big ladle and dipped it in again. I carefully put some of the stew into the bowl on his tray. It actually did smell good. I repeated the process and the second scoop filled the bowl to the brim. The man reached out and grabbed a bun.

"Thanks," he said.

"You're welcome. I hope it's good."

"Guaranteed to be the *best* thing I eat today," he said and then chuckled. "Guaranteed to be the *only* thing I eat today."

"I'm ... I'm ... sorry," I stammered.

"Not your fault," he said and shrugged.

"Maybe you could take another bun or—"

He shook his head. "Can't do that. Might be taking the last bun away from somebody who gets nothing. Maybe at the end when you get some stew I'll get an extra bun."

"Sure ... okay."

This really hadn't been what I'd expected. This guy hadn't even eaten today, and he was worried about somebody at the back of the line he probably didn't even know. That wasn't how I was expecting a street person to be.

"You two through gabbing?" barked the man behind him. "There are people here who need some grub, you know."

I startled and then quickly dipped the ladle into the pot. I fished out a heaping helping and as I dropped it into the bowl it slopped onto the tray.

"Be careful!" he barked. "Don't go wasting my food!"

"Sorry, it was an accident."

He was older and grizzled and there was more than just a *slight* odour of alcohol coming off him. He seemed to be swaying back and forth ever so gently, and as I carefully put a second scoop into his bowl I saw that the tray was shaking.

"You can take a bun," I said.

"You think I don't know the routine!" he snapped. "I've been coming here longer than you've been alive, you little—"

"Leave him alone, you old buzzard!" snapped the first man I'd served.

"You want a piece of me?" challenged the old man. "You hassle me and I'll cut ya!"

"Take your food, shut up, and sit down!" It was Mac. "You say another word and you'll be banned for two weeks!"

The old man opened his mouth to answer, revealing a mess of yellowed and missing teeth. He mumbled something under his breath, but turned and walked away, sitting down at the table with his back to us.

"Don't worry about it," Mac said to me. "You didn't do nothing wrong. Just keep serving."

I dipped the ladle back into the pot and served out food to the next man in line and then the next and the next. It was funny, every one of them was the same but different. Some were polite, others rude, some were like zombies, hardly noticing that I'd given them food until they were prodded by the person behind them to keep moving. There were those who were cursing under their breath or muttering away, talking to people I couldn't see or hear answer back. Some were angry. Others seemed cheerful, even happy. Maybe they were the craziest of the bunch. Wouldn't you have to be crazy to be happy eating at a soup kitchen and living on the street? There were some who didn't seem that much older than me, others who must have been in their seventies, and a whole bunch whose ages I couldn't discern behind the layers of grime, beard, and clothing. They could have been twenty-seven or seventy-two. Interestingly, there wasn't a woman in the group. Where did the shopping cart lady go to eat? Was there another soup kitchen for women?

I got to the bottom of the first pot. I was just going to put it aside when I looked back at the line. It was at least as long as when I'd started serving. What would happen if there wasn't enough food for the last few in line? I wasn't so worried about them going hungry as how they might react—how they might react to *me*—if they didn't get fed. What was that saying I'd heard about delivering bad news? *Kill the messenger* ... that was it. I'd be the guy to tell them there was no more food. That old man had mentioned cutting somebody and if the man in the park was to be believed everybody in here had some sort of weapon. That is, everybody in here but *me*.

I tipped the pot and scraped the stew off the side, accumulating it until there was a full ladle to dish out.

"That's the way you do it," Mac said. He had returned from the kitchen carrying more buns.

I put the now completely empty pot off to the side and dragged forward the second pot. I took off the lid. The stew was still steamy hot. Maybe I was hungrier than I thought because it did still smell good to me. I dipped in the ladle and added a second scoop to the bowl of the man patiently waiting. He smiled and nodded his head in thanks.

I caught a quick glimpse of my watch. I'd been here less than forty minutes. It seemed like hours already.

"Do we have enough?" I asked Mac, motioning toward the back of the line.

"I think we'll be okay. Hopefully enough that we get a bowl too. You already eaten?" Mac asked.

"I grabbed something before I left home," I answered. That something was a granola bar and a couple of cookies. I didn't care how good the stew smelled, or how hungry I was, there was no way I was going to eat here.

"You lyin' to me?" Mac asked.

"What?"

"You lyin' about eating?"

"No, of course not," I lied.

"Just wanted to make sure. Didn't want you to lie so you wouldn't be taking food away from some of our clients. We won't be taking food from somebody. We'll only eat once everybody has had their fill."

"It's just that I'm not hungry ... honestly."

"How can you not be hungry for a bowl of this?" Mac asked in all seriousness. "It's my own recipe, made from only the finest ingredients."

"Where do you get all this food from?" I asked, trying to change the subject.

"Some I have to buy, but a whole lot of it comes from Second Harvest."

"What's that?" I asked as I continued to serve the people in line.

"It's an organization that picks up food from stores and restaurants that have extra. It's all perfectly good food that would go to waste if it wasn't collected and put to good use. The meat for our stew today is cut-up steak from Centros."

"Centros!"

"You know it?" he asked.

"Who doesn't? Centros is one of the classiest, most expensive restaurants in town."

"Never been there myself, but that's what I hear."

I'd been there half a dozen times with my parents. I thought it was best not to mention that.

"But why would they give away food?"

"Sometimes they order too much, or there's problems with the freezer, or the chef just doesn't think it's tender enough. Maybe they just want to do something good. Anyway you cut it, they get a charitable donation receipt and we get to feed some people who really need to be fed."

Just then there was a commotion over in the corner. Two men, sitting across from each other at a table, had jumped to their feet and were yelling and swearing at each other. It looked like it was going to evolve into a full-fledged fist fight.

"Excuse me," Mac said. He reached by me under the counter and pulled out a big black baseball bat! I backed away.

Mac moved around the counter and quickly got close to where the two men were screaming at each other. What was he going to do with that bat? Without warning he smashed the bat down on the table between the two men, causing cups to overturn and bowls and cutlery to jump along the whole length of the table!

"Both of you, sit down or get out!" he yelled at the top of his lungs.

The whole room had gone completely silent. Everybody had stopped eating or talking; they all stared at Mac holding the bat. Both men dropped back down to their seats without saying another word.

"How you act on the streets is your business!" Mac said sternly. "How you act in here is mine! I don't know what you were fighting about, but I want you both to forget it. Shake hands and be friends."

I expected them to argue or get up and leave. Instead they held out their hands and shook.

"That's better," Mac said. "We'll have no more of this ... from anybody." He looked around the room, holding the bat up. "Isn't life tough enough for us already? Aren't there enough people out there trying to harm and abuse you without doing it to each other?"

A couple of men called out in agreement and others nodded their heads. Mac walked back over, circled the counter, and put the bat away underneath it. The regular sounds of the room—talking, laughing, clinking of cutlery and bowls and glasses all started up again. It was like the whole thing had never taken place.

"Does that happen very often?" I asked.

"Too often for my liking, but not as much as in the past. I'm known to run a pretty strict place here. Those who aren't gonna follow the rules know better than to come here."

"If they don't come here where do they go instead?" I asked, hoping to avoid that place completely.

"This isn't the only location in town offering a meal. Of course, some people have been banned from some places and others don't ever come to soup kitchens to begin with."

"What do they do instead?" I asked.

"Eat out of dumpsters, hang around the streets or the park just over from here begging for change." He paused. "That park is one bad place."

Again I was tempted to say something but I held my tongue. I didn't know why I cared what he thought but I did. Maybe it was nothing more than me not wanting him to think I was an idiot or a wimp. I just kept on ladling out stew. If we did run out of food, at least I knew where the baseball bat was now.

Three

MAC GENTLY SHEPHERDED OUT the last of the men. As they'd
eaten, people had become more animated and talkative and some had
wanted to stay and talk to Mac. The very last few stragglers had been the
most reluctant to leave. I guess I couldn't blame them. This wasn't the
fanciest place in the world but at least it was warm and dry and inside.
Mac said goodbye to the last man, closed the door and bolted it shut.

I continued to gather up bowls and cups, piling them up on a tray.
I put two more bowls on the tray. It was now as full as I dared to carry.
I hefted it up and carted it away, pushing through the swinging door
and into the kitchen. It smelled better back here—smells of hot water
and cooking odours. Out in the dining room the men were gone but
their smell lingered on. Through the course of the evening, the smell
of the food had been replaced by a foul combination of dirt and sweat
and urine that stung my nostrils. It was so strong that it was more a
taste than an smell.

On my first trip into the kitchen I'd been shocked to find out that
nobody else was in the back helping. I'd figured that there had to be at
least a couple of other people. There was nobody else. It had all been

Mac and me—really Mac. If I hadn't showed up he would have done the whole thing by himself.

The counter was already overflowing with dirty dishes and I put down the tray carefully so as not to disturb the rest of the mess. The sink, filled with soapy suds, was already filled to capacity. Was I supposed to help wash the dishes as well? I hated washing dishes—not that I did it very often. Berta, our housekeeper, took care of all those things. If I was supposed to do the dishes here that could take forever. Then again, what did I care? The longer I was here the more quickly I'd be through having to come back. It was seven forty-five. If I worked another fifteen minutes that would be two hours. That meant I had to come here *twenty* times to complete my placement. If I came here three times a week that would take almost seven weeks. If I hadn't been so stupid I would have started doing my hours when everybody else did. It would probably be better if I did stay and work on the dishes. If I stayed until nine that would be three hours, and I'd only have to come here thirteen times—only thirteen times. I shook my head.

I dipped my hands into the hot water and fished around for the dishcloth. I swirled it around the first bowl—the first of how many bowls? I didn't even want to count them. Satisfied that the first bowl was clean, I dipped it into the second sink, which was filled with clear water, and rinsed off the remaining suds.

"You don't have to do that," Mac said as he entered the kitchen carrying more dishes.

"Somebody's got to do it," I said and shrugged.

"That somebody's usually me."

"Do you do everything around here?" I asked as I pulled out another bowl.

"I'm the executive director, the chief cook, the bouncer and bottle washer." He set the tray down. "Although sometimes I have more help than I want."

"What do you mean?"

"Sometimes there's a tidal wave of do-gooders who show up. They can cause more damage than they do good. You didn't do half bad tonight," he said as he continued to stack bowls.

"So does that mean I did half good?"

"Don't push it. What that means is you didn't screw up and that means you can come back again."

"Gee, thanks, what an honour."

"Maybe you *should* consider it an honour. Lots of people I don't ask to come back. You done okay. You served the food, you didn't ask too many questions, you were polite, and like I said, you were here for the same reason as everybody else—you had no choice ... same as everybody we fed tonight. I never met anybody who said his dream was to live on the streets, beg for change, wonder where his next meal was gonna come from, or where he was going to sleep." He dropped more bowls in the sink. "If you didn't have to do this for school, is there any way in the world you'd be here tonight?"

I laughed. "Yeah, right, like washing dishes is my dream job."

"That's another thing I like about you," he said. "You're honest."

I didn't know what to say to that. I didn't know if my parents or most of my teachers would have thought that about me.

"What about you?" I asked. "Do *you* want to be here?"

"This is the place I'm *supposed* to be."

I guess I looked confused, because that was how I felt.

"This is my calling."

"You sound like a priest or minister or something," I said. I focused on the dishes in the sink, not wanting to look at him as the conversation got more serious.

"Maybe I am."

"You are?"

"Don't sound so surprised. Don't I seem like a minister?" he asked, a serious look on his face.

I thought about the minister at our church—the church we went to at Christmas and Easter and maybe two other times a year. He was always dressed immaculately, with a sharp crease in his pants, drove a fancy car, and lived in the big beautiful house beside the church. Sometimes my father would go golfing with him at the country club. I could picture our minister on the golf course, and I could clearly see him standing up at the altar boring me with another sermon. What I couldn't do was imagine him making stew or cleaning tables. I certainly couldn't, in my *wildest* dreams, picture him pulling out a baseball bat to stop a fight between two of the parishioners.

"Well?" Mac asked.

"Not really," I admitted, hoping I wasn't insulting him.

"I'll take that as a compliment," he said as his serious expression dissolved into a crooked smile. "I'm not part of any church or anything like that, but this is my mission. God is everywhere. Here," he said, motioning with his hands. "And out there on the streets."

I don't know which streets he'd been on but the ones I'd walked down today looked like God had forgotten them and the people who lived on them.

"How long have you been doing this?" I asked, turning away from the soapy sink.

"It's coming up to ten years I've been running the place. Seven days a week."

"Seven days a week?" I asked in amazement. "Don't you get any time off?"

"People need to eat seven days a week. I'll take a day off when hunger does. This is my place ... literally." He pointed to a bed in the corner.

"You mean you live here?" I asked incredulously.

"Saves on the commute and the rent is perfect. I've slept in a lot worse places."

I wanted to ask him what could possibly be worse than this, but I didn't want to offend him. I kept washing dishes, rinsing them off, and piling them on the counter. Mac took each one, dried it off, and put it in the cupboard. There didn't seem to be an end to the bowls.

"How many people you figure were here tonight?" I asked. "It must have been close to a hundred."

"One hundred and seven," he said. "I have to do a head count. Our funding is based on the number of people that get fed."

"I thought the food came from fancy restaurants."

"That and food donations from all over, but they don't pay the rent, or my salary, or guarantee there's food on the table every night. We get some funds from the government and some from the United Way. These people need food every night."

"I had no idea there were that many homeless in the city. One hundred and seven seems like a lot," I said.

"That's just a little drop in the bucket. Those are the people who showed up here tonight. It doesn't include them who skipped a meal, or went to another soup kitchen, or got their meal from a dumpster behind McDonald's, or were too drunk to show up, or who were spending the night in jail or in an emergency department of a hospital, or who were off their medication and couldn't stand to be around other people," he said, counting the reasons off on his fingers.

"Then how many people—homeless people—do you think there are in the city?"

"It varies from month to month, mostly depending on the season, and whether you count kids who run away for a day or two," he explained.

"Right now, *tonight,* how many people do you think are out there on the streets looking for a place to sleep?" I didn't know why but it seemed important to me.

He didn't answer right away. I could tell he was thinking. "My guess is well over a thousand … maybe two thousand."

"That can't be right," I argued. "Sure, I see some street people around but there can't be two thousand."

"You don't live around here, do you?"

I shook my head. "About a thirty-minute drive away in the suburbs." I wanted to say in another universe but I didn't.

"Not many street people where you live, I bet. Lots here if you know where to look. You'd see 'em too, if you went out with me on my rounds."

"Your rounds?"

"I walk through the streets and alleys and parks, talking to people, letting them know about the kitchen here, and suggest places where they might want to sleep."

"Is that a safe thing to do?" My experience in the park came flooding back.

"It's safe … for me. I know pretty well everybody. It's not like I'm a stranger."

"I guess you really do get to know a lot of them," I said, remembering how he greeted people at the door this evening as they came in.

"I know a lot of them," he repeated in agreement. "I even understand them … well, at least some of them. You know, we're all the same in so many ways, but I don't pretend to know the demons that some people live with. You can walk a mile in somebody's shoes but those shoes still belong to them." He paused. "It's getting late. How are you getting home?"

I hadn't really thought about it. "I guess I should call and ask my mother to pick me up."

"Then why don't you call now. By the time we get finished she should be here. The phone is right over there."

I dried my hands on the apron and walked over to the phone.

"And tell her to make sure she keeps all the car doors locked," Mac said.

That sounded like good advice.

Four

THE SOUND OF THE CHALK squeaking against the board brought me out of my thoughts and back into the classroom. Mrs. Watkins was writing something. I'd been trying my best to block her out all class but she had the same grating effect as the chalk. She seemed to know just what to say or how to say it to stop me from drifting off too often. Maybe that was a good quality for a teacher to have but it certainly cut down on my ability to catch up on my sleep.

It had been late when I got to bed and even later when I finally drifted off. My mind was filled with all the images I'd seen the night before. My mother would have called it processing. Leave it to her to put everything in computer terms instead of human terms—computers she knew about. I lay in bed thinking about the lady with the shopping cart, the men shuffling in for their meal, the conversations—angry, crazy, polite—and the smells of the food and the alcohol and the body odours. And I realized how close I came to not only losing my shoes, but maybe having the crap beaten out of me, and wondering what could have happened if that man hadn't stopped them.

Mrs. Watkins moved aside to reveal the words she had written on the board. In big letters they read, *Peacekeepers, not War Makers*.

"Does anybody know what that means?" she asked.

"It probably means more work for us," a voice shot out from the back of the room and a number of people laughed in response.

"Anybody else care to add something ... something of value?" she asked.

Nobody raised a hand or a voice.

"Does the name Lester B. Pearson mean anything?" Mrs. Watkins asked.

"Didn't he used to play for the Leafs?" the same guy—Jeremy—asked and there was more laughter.

"Somebody better come up with an answer or everybody is going to be given an additional assignment on Canadian prime ministers," she threatened.

"Okay, he was a Canadian prime minister," somebody answered.

"And he is best known for?" Mrs. Watkins questioned.

Obviously he wasn't best known for much of anything because nobody even knew who he was.

Mrs. Watkins let out a big, deep sigh. "Let's try this from another angle. In the rest of the world what is *Canada* known for? What are the symbols or institutions or objects that the world thinks of when it thinks of Canada and Canadians?"

"Hockey," several people called out.

"We're the best in the world on the ice. Everybody knows that," Jeremy said.

"What else?" Mrs. Watkins asked.

"Maple syrup and the Mounties," somebody else volunteered.

"Universal health care," Kelsey added.

"All sorts of programs including medicine, pensions, and education," Mrs. Watkins said, nodding. "What else?"

"The paint roller," a boy—Justin—offered.

"Paint roller?" the kid behind me repeated, sounding amused.

"A Canadian invented it," the first boy explained and shrugged.

"All valid. Now, what else?" Mrs. Watkins asked.

"Snow and cold and igloos and Eskimos," another girl added.

"Niagara Falls and the mountains," another voice added.

"All good. And are we seen as a country that believes in war?"

"I hope not," somebody said, "because I don't think we even have an army."

"We have armed forces. Not large but very professional and well respected," Mrs. Watkins said. "The question was, do we believe in war?"

"We were in both world wars," Kelsey said hesitantly.

"We were a major player," Mrs. Watkins confirmed. "And there was the Korean War and the Gulf War, but the question isn't have we *been* in wars but do we *believe* in war?" Mrs. Watkins said. "What do you think, Ian?"

I jumped at the mention of my name. That was one of her annoying, chalk-like qualities, calling out your name when you thought you were being left alone.

"Well?" she asked, looking directly at me.

"I'm not really sure ... but I guess not really. We're peaceful," I said. I looked at the words looking back at me on the board. "We're peacekeepers not war makers."

"Exactly!" she exclaimed. "Now who was Lester B. Pearson?"

"I thought we'd answered that one already," Justin said. "He was a prime minister."

"But what else?" she demanded.

"Maybe he was the one who started us being peacekeepers," I offered.

"Right again!" Mrs. Watkins exclaimed. "He put forward a plan, when he was foreign minister, to send peacekeepers to the Middle

East. These peacekeepers were almost all Canadians and they separated the two warring sides, averting a war in the Suez. And after the
success of this first mission he created the legacy of peacekeeping
that has marked Canada's role on the international scene and saved
literally hundreds of thousands of lives around the world."

That did sound impressive ... well, not to me, but I'm sure to
some people.

"For his efforts he was awarded the Nobel Prize for Peace in 1957,"
she continued. "He was subsequently elected by the United Nations
as—" Her words were cut off by the loud ringing of the bell marking
the end of class. Everybody, en masse, grabbed their books and bags
and rose to their feet.

"I want everybody to read their textbooks, pages 145 to 155
tonight!" Mrs. Watkins yelled out over the din. "There just might be a
test tomorrow!"

I'd try and remember—maybe I should write it down. There was
no point in doing these volunteer hours if I didn't at least pass the
rest of the course. I pulled out my pen and started to write myself
a reminder on my hand.

"You should try using paper," Mrs. Watkins suggested. "It's a
wonderful new invention. I think it was the Chinese created it ...
about three thousand years ago."

"At least I'm writing it down," I replied.

"I guess you're right. So how did things go at your placement ...
you did go, didn't you?" she asked.

"I went and things went okay."

"Just okay?"

"The placement was fine. It was just that it was, I don't know,
different."

"Different as in not what you are used to or not what you were
expecting?"

"Both."

"I'm sure it was all pretty overwhelming."

I nodded. "It was. It all just kept going around and around in my head after I left. I even had trouble concentrating in class today."

"Well, at least you had a valid excuse for not concentrating today." She smiled. "Cheap shot. Seriously, it really is a different world out there, isn't it?"

"Not a different world. A different *universe*."

"That's what this course is designed to do, to open your mind up to other perspectives. So when do you go back?" she asked.

"Friday night. I'm going to help with set-up, then dinner, then help clean up."

"If you need to talk about things, feel free to give me a call," she said.

"A call ... like on the phone?"

"That would be the right way. I'm in the book if you need to talk."

"You want me to call you at home?" This was all very strange. I didn't even think she liked me and now she was offering to let me call her at home. I got the feeling that a whole lot of teachers didn't even want to talk to me when I was in class.

"A big part of my course is asking you to move beyond the classroom. It would be very hypocritical of me to ask you to do that while I stayed safely within the confines of my class. If you need to call, then call."

"I'll be fine."

"I'm sure you'll handle it." She paused for a few seconds. "Just remember, a sign of strength is asking for help."

Strength or weakness, it didn't matter because I wasn't going to be calling her at home.

"I've got to tell you that I was most impressed, and somewhat surprised, with your decision to pursue that particular placement.

Most kids went for the easy stuff—reading to kids in a local elementary school, or going to the humane society to walk dogs, or even visiting seniors at the local nursing home."

She'd described most of the placements my friends were doing.

"Not that there's anything wrong with those placements," she said. "They all make a contribution. What you're doing, though, is different. Almost noble. Now you better get going or you're going to be late for your next class."

Five

"ARE YOU SURE you have to do this?" my mother asked as we drove along.

"Are you sure you want me to pass civics?"

"There have to be more pleasant places in a better part of town where you could have done your hours."

I had to agree that *pleasant* and *better* certainly weren't words that I'd use to describe either the soup kitchen or the streets that surrounded it.

"I started it so I'm going to finish it."

"I just wish you hadn't started it working at a place like that."

That would have been my wish as well—unfortunately most of what I wished for didn't come true. At least one of the few benefits this placement had was that it offended my mother. She always liked things to be so proper. So precise, so tidy and organized. This was none of those things. That it bothered my mother almost made up for me having to give up a Friday night—almost. I'd rather be out with my friends but I had to do the hours as soon as possible.

It was a shame I didn't get credit for the time I'd spent thinking about the soup kitchen or I'd have already been through with my community hours. I couldn't get it out of my mind. And the more I thought about it, the less real it all seemed. It was like I'd watched a movie about it instead of actually being there.

Tonight I was dressed better. By that, I mean I dressed *worse*—old coat, as close to beat up as I could find. It sort of belonged to my father. It was what he used to wear when he did yard work—at least when he used to do yard work. It had been years since he'd cut the grass or raked leaves or shovelled the snow. Now there was a landscape company that did all of that. And another company that took care of the pools, and another that washed the windows. He was far too busy—and too important—to do any of those jobs. Now if he could just find somebody to parent, he wouldn't have to show up at all.

I had also dug up an old pair of sneakers. They were scuffed up and worn out. I was sure nobody would want to steal them, and if they did I'd gladly give them up without a fight.

"I still don't know why you couldn't have dressed a bit better," my mother said, repeating the refrain I'd heard since she first saw my outfit.

"Like I said, it's better to dress down. If I look like I might have money, then somebody might want to try and get that money from me."

"Then by all means just give them a dollar or two so they'll leave you alone," she said. "Your father always gives those squeegee kids a dollar so they won't scratch up his car. It's not like we can't afford it."

"Can we afford for me to have my wallet ripped off, or my shoes or jacket stolen, or for me to be bashed over the head?"

"Please, Ian, don't be so dramatic."

"I'm *not* being ... Fine ... whatever."

I was tempted to tell her what had happened the other night in the park, but I stopped myself. I'd save that for later and spring it on her at just the right time.

"And it's such a long distance from home, such a long way to drive," she said.

"Sorry to inconvenience you," I said icily.

"It's not that."

"You don't even have to drive me. I can get there and back on my own. If it's such a big hassle, I can take the subway home tonight."

"Not from this part of the city and certainly not at night."

I was so happy she said that. I'd only been bluffing. A drive was a lot nicer, and safer. They'd just have to keep driving me places until I got my licence and my own car—that was the reason I was going in the first place. It was important not to lose sight of that.

"You can let me off anywhere along here," I suggested. We were within a block now.

"I'll drop you off right out front where I picked you up the other night. I'd rather not have you on these streets by yourself."

"I can take care of myself."

"You think you can take care of yourself, but you have no idea what goes on in this part of town."

"Sure, fine, whatever."

Actually I was a little embarrassed to be driven up to a soup kitchen in a Mercedes that probably cost more than all the meals that had been served there for the past year.

I grabbed a toque off the seat and pulled it low over my head. It was an old ratty one and it was a tight fit ... although it certainly would help me fit in down here. Was it some sort of rule that every street person had to wear a toque?

My mother pulled the car over to the curb directly in front of the building. There was no lineup in front—I'd been hoping that was the case. It was still early—not even five o'clock—and I was here to help with the set-up.

"You'd think they could do something about this place," my mother said. "Fix it up a little or—"

"They spend their money on other things ... like food for the street people."

"I just think a little bit of paint wouldn't cost much and it would certainly improve the image."

"Appearances don't mean that much down here," I said.

"Judging from *your* appearance that's pretty obvious."

"I think they believe it isn't what you look like, but what you do." I opened the car door and climbed out.

"Call when you know what time—"

I slammed the door shut, using the fine German engineering of the car to close *her* out. I turned and walked away without looking back. I'd gone no more than a few steps when I heard the car pull away, leaving behind a small squeal of rubber on the pavement. She was obviously mad. Good. It shouldn't just be me who was mad all the time.

I grabbed the handle of the door to the Club and tried to pull it open. It rattled but didn't open. I knocked. It echoed loudly. I waited, listening for an answer. There was none. I knocked again. This time louder and longer. Still nothing. I'd be awfully ticked off if I'd come down here early—like we'd agreed—and Mac wasn't here. Either way, though, whether I was in there working or out here standing, I was still counting this as volunteer hours. I knocked again. No answer. Either Mac wasn't here or he was just ignoring the noise. He probably got a lot of people pounding on the door wanting to get inside to eat. It wasn't like most of the homeless people had watches. Maybe there was another way in.

I circled around to the alley at the side of the building. I'd gone no more than a few feet when I was stopped in my tracks by the sight of two legs sticking out from beside a dumpster. Was somebody dead or ... I gave my head a shake. It was probably just somebody waiting for supper. They would have figured this was a good place to get out of the wind. I walked forward, angling out and away from that side of the alley. I glanced over and then stopped for a better look.

It was an old man, sitting on the ground, leaning against the wall, his eyes closed, a half-empty bottle in his hand. As I stood there, he opened one eye and looked at me. He mumbled something I couldn't hear and then his eye fell shut again. He certainly wasn't dead. Not unless you counted dead drunk.

As I got to the end of the alley I saw a large truck, backed in so it was tucked close to the open rear door of the building. At that instant Mac came out through the door and grabbed a box from the back of the truck. He looked up, saw me, and waved.

"Just in time!" he called out. "Grab a box!"

I rushed over. The truck was piled high with crates and cardboard boxes and bins. I picked one up.

"What's in all of these?" I asked.

"This is a place where people come to get food ... so ..."

"This is all food?"

"Bingo!"

I trailed after Mac, and as we entered the building a man came out.

"Extra hands is good," he said. He had on a shirt emblazoned with Second Harvest Trucking on the front so I assumed he was the driver.

Mac set his box down on the table that was already piled high with other boxes. I went to put mine down when he stopped me.

"That one goes in the freezer. Follow me, I'll show you."

Mac led the way to a large metal door. He opened it up and gestured for me to enter. I was immediately hit with a wave of cold. It was a gigantic walk-in freezer. The walls were lined with shelves and the shelves were filled with boxes and cartons and containers.

"Put it right here," Mac said.

"There's a whole lot of food in here."

"Enough for eight or nine days."

"There's got to be more than that."

"Second time here and the kid thinks he's an expert," Mac said.

"No, it's just that—"

Mac started laughing, his breath coming out in little white puffs in the cold. "You gotta lighten up, kid. I was just pulling your leg."

We walked out of the freezer and he closed the door behind us with a loud metallic click.

"It takes a lot of food to feed more than a hundred men a day," Mac said. "A lot of food and a whole lot of work. Glad to see you here to help. Although I'm a little surprised."

"Why are you surprised? This is when I'm supposed to be here, right?"

"That's the time we agreed to, but lots of people who show up once don't show up again. Especially people who aren't used to this sort of thing ... people who come from privilege."

"What makes you think that's me?" I asked.

"Well, for starters, the way you were dressed last time in that expensive coat and shoes. You made a better choice this time," he said.

"I thought I could fit in better this way," I admitted, feeling a bit embarrassed. "But lots of people own a coat like the one I was wearing. That doesn't mean my family is rich."

"Maybe not the coat, but certainly the Mercedes that picked you up. That one probably cost more than a hundred grand, right?"

I nodded my head. It was one of the top-of-the-line cars. But how did he know what sort of car picked me up? Had he been spying on me?

"I was watching when you left, peeking out the window, to make sure you got picked up safe," Mac said, answering my unspoken thoughts.

"Doesn't matter what car picked me up or dropped me off," I said, feeling a bit defensive. "All that matters is that I have to put in my hours, so I'm here."

Mac laughed. "Like I said before, that's one of the things I like about you, kid. You aren't going to give me some crap about helping the poor. You're here to do a job. Honest. I like that. But you know, there are other places where you could have done your hours. You could have weaseled out of being here."

"That's what my mother wanted me to do."

"But you didn't do what she wanted. How come?"

I considered giving him a completely honest answer; I hardly ever did what my mother or father wanted unless I had no choice. "I told you I'd be here so I'm here," I said. That wasn't a complete lie.

"Good. How about if you continue unloading the truck while I finish up making supper. Unless you want to do the cooking and I'll do the unloading?"

"I think I'll do the unloading. Lifting I know how to do. Cooking for a hundred people I don't."

"Same as cooking for two people. Just multiply all the ingredients by fifty."

I went out to continue unloading. Each time I came in with a box I caught a glimpse of Mac working at the stove. It wasn't just that I didn't know how to cook for one hundred people. I didn't know how to cook for two. Or even one. I'd never needed to. Berta did all of that.

Berta was my nanny when I was a baby, and then when I didn't need a nanny any more she became our housekeeper and organizer. She had an apartment in our basement and she was always there. My mother said Berta was sort of like the family's *wife* who took care of all the day-to-day business of running our household. I didn't think of her as anybody's wife, but she was family. She'd always been there. She was there when I came home from school. Because of her, the house was never empty, and because my father and mother were always so busy with business meetings and travel and of course social things, it *would* have been empty without her. Filled with lots of expensive things—but empty. I couldn't even imagine what it would be like without Berta around—thank goodness I'd never known and I'd never have to know.

I guess it also worked out for Berta. She was originally from Guatemala and that's where all her family still lived, so I guess in some ways we were like her family too.

I'd once started to figure out how often I ate with my parents and how often it was just me and Berta for dinner. I looked back for two or three weeks and then stopped. There was no point in quantifying what I already knew. Not that there was anything wrong with eating with Berta. I liked eating with her. I liked being with her.

She had a soft, gentle laugh, and she always seemed to know what questions to ask and, just as important, what questions not to ask. Those were the times I told her the rest of the story anyway. I knew I could trust her. She didn't judge me, although she did offer advice— softly spoken with her lilting accent. I loved her accent. My parents told me that when I was little I spoke English with a Spanish accent. That shouldn't have been a surprise since she'd spent more time with me than my mother did.

"Much more to go?" Mac asked.

"Almost done."

"Good. When you're finished, you can start bringing out the plates and cups and utensils."

"Sure. By the way, what's for supper tonight?" I asked.

"Spaghetti with meat sauce." Mac lifted the lid on the biggest pot I'd ever seen. He grabbed a wooden spoon—a spoon that was about the same size as a canoe paddle—and stirred the bright red sauce that was bubbling away. He needed to use both hands to move the contents.

"I make sure there's lots and lots of vegetables in the sauce," Mac said. "Best thing to protect 'em from getting scurvy."

"Scurvy? Isn't that what sailors got in the old days ... you know ... like Christopher Columbus?"

"Yep. Being at sea for a long time without fruits and vegetables does that."

"And street people get it?" I asked.

"They don't get what you'd call a balanced diet. Speaking of which, have you eaten?" Mac asked.

I hadn't and it was too early to claim I had. I shook my head.

"Finish up and I'll set out two bowls before we let the crowd in. Okay?"

"You sure there'll be enough for everybody?" I asked.

"There will be, but that's mighty nice of you to ask."

I WAS IN CHARGE of serving the spaghetti. I was using a big pair of serving tongs. Mac was putting on the sauce. His job was way easier. The noodles were hard to get out of the pot and onto the plate. It almost seemed like they were alive and struggling to stay in the pot so they wouldn't be eaten. And when I did convince the noodles to leave, it was hard to get just the right amount, the right serving size. If I put on too much, I couldn't very well reach out and take it back, and if I didn't put out enough, I could get somebody mad. It was much simpler serving the stew the other night—two scoops, plop, plop.

An old grizzled man stood in front of me, tray in hand.

I wondered how old he was. I was finding that everybody looked old and worn. He could have been fifty but he could have been one hundred and fifty.

"Is it any good?" he asked.

"It's really good," I answered. It was good enough for me to have eaten two full servings.

"It don't smell right."

I thought it smelled pretty good. "It's the garlic in the sauce you're smelling."

"They put somethin' in the sauce?" he asked.

"There's lots of things. Garlic, green peppers, onions and—"

"Says who?" the old man demanded.

"Well … me, I guess."

"And who are you and who do you work for?" the old man snapped.

I didn't know what to say. The old man started to snarl, his teeth—those that he had—yellowed and crooked and grubby, were locked together in a fierce-looking grimace, and he started to make a strange noise. Was he growling?

"What did you put in that sauce?" he yelled. He raised his fist and started shaking it toward me.

I backed a half step away. I felt a rush of adrenaline surge through my body. I realized that everybody had stopped talking or shuffling or eating and all eyes were on us.

"I didn't put anything in the—"

"It's okay," Mac said, stepping forward and cutting me off.

"How do I know it ain't poisoned?" the old man demanded. "How do I know this ain't another plot to get me and everybody else in here?" He gestured around the room.

"Come on, buddy, you've been coming here a long time. You know I wouldn't poison you or let anybody else poison you," Mac reasoned. "You *know* me."

The old man stopped growling and he lowered his fist. Those had to be good signs. He looked at Mac, long and hard, like he was trying to figure out if what he was saying was true. His grimace dissolved into a twisted, broken smile like he'd suddenly realized that it was Mac. I felt myself relax.

That had looked like it was going to end really bad, and Mac had managed to handle it so that—

"How do I know it's you?" the old man demanded. "How do I know they didn't kill the *real* Mac and replace him with you when they poisoned the food? How do I know you're not an alien!" he yelled. He raised his fist and started to growl again. If he wasn't so old and frail and if Mac wasn't here I would have been afraid. Actually, I was afraid. I'd never seen anybody this crazy this close up.

"Would I poison myself?" Mac said, his voice calm and quiet. He reached into the pot and grabbed a noodle, stuffing it in his mouth. Next he took a spoon, dipped it in the sauce, and took a sample.

"See?" Mac said.

Once again the man lowered his fist and the growling was replaced by a throaty, scratchy laugh.

"Mac ... it's you ... right?"

"Who else would be stupid enough to be here, you old buzzard?"

The old man held out his hand and they shook.

"Go ahead," Mac said, "serve him."

The old man held out his tray. Carefully, very carefully, I put on some spaghetti.

"Thank you so much, young man," he said sweetly.

Next Mac poured on sauce—giving him an extra big serving—and the man shuffled off to eat.

"Thanks," I said to Mac.

"No problem. That's why I'm here. Sometimes you just gotta enter their heads and figure out what they're thinking."

"I can't believe that. He actually thought you were an alien. An alien who was here to poison him."

"That's why I had to sample the sauce to prove him wrong," Mac explained.

"But what I don't understand is if he thought you were an alien, isn't it possible that what poisons humans isn't going to hurt an alien?" I asked.

"Ssshhhhhh!" Mac hissed. "Let's not give anybody else any ideas!"

"That's good advice," another voice said.

I looked up to the man standing in front of me holding out his tray. It was the man from the park!

"Good to see you!" Mac exclaimed and the two men shook hands over the counter. "Haven't seen you for a while. Good to have you back. How've you been?" Mac asked.

"I'm fine. More important, how is your food today?"

"Good as always," Mac said. "See for yourself. Ian, give the Sarge a big serving 'cause he's a big guy."

"The same as everybody else would be fine," he said softly.

I pulled out a blob of spaghetti. As it had been getting colder it had become increasingly more difficult to manage. Whether he wanted it or not, he was getting a bigger serving.

"Thank you. I see you have on a different jacket today. I trust that was a choice and not something forced on you."

"I thought it was smarter to wear this when I'm around the neighbourhood."

"Wise move."

"Do you two know each other?" Mac asked.

"We met briefly in the park," the man said. "He kindly offered me some spare change. He's a nice young man."

"Yeah, I think he's a keeper," Mac said.

"I'm sure he is. *Merci* to you both." He nodded his head and then walked off looking for a seat. I watched as he walked. There was no shuffle or stagger in his step. His back was as straight as a rod. He looked more like he was marching than walking.

"You called him Sarge," I said.

"That's what everybody calls him. It's not his name. That's just what we call him. He was in the army before is what I heard."

That would explain the way he walked, the way he held himself— the way he knocked that man down and wielded that iron bar.

"So he was a sergeant?"

"Might have been," Mac said with a shrug. "He gets called Sarge the way somebody who used to drive a taxi might be called Cabby. Everybody here has a nickname and a story," Mac said.

"And what's his story?" I asked.

"What I know I'll tell you sometime." Mac paused. "That is, if you tell me the rest of the story about you and him meeting. I get the feeling that there's more there."

I nodded my head. "It's a deal."

Six

I REMOVED THE STOPPER from the sink and the water started to swirl away. I pulled off the bright yellow gloves that Mac had made me wear. He'd said that if I was going to be here on a regular basis he didn't want me filing a workman's compensation complaint about having dishpan hands.

"You all finished in here?" Mac yelled out.

"Pretty well. You?" He'd been working out front sweeping and wiping the tables and getting things ready for tomorrow's meal.

"All done. So you got a ride home?" he asked.

"I'll call to arrange it." I paused. "You were going to tell me about that man ... Sarge."

"Not tonight."

"Why not?" I asked.

"Not enough time."

"I could tell them to pick me up later."

"Not your time, mine. I've got to get going."

"You got a big date?" I asked.

"I should be so lucky. I'm heading out onto the streets to do my rounds."

"What exactly do you do out there?" I asked.

"Hard to explain, really." He hesitated. "But I could show you some time ... if you were interested in coming along."

"Sure, that would be good," I answered. I was interested, but also more than a little uneasy. Going out there would be a little like riding a roller coaster or watching a scary movie—neither of which I liked doing.

"You know, it would give you hours on your community service." Mac knew which buttons to push.

"I could come tonight," I said. The words had jumped out before I'd thought them through.

"It'll be almost midnight before I'm through," he warned.

"It's a Friday night. I don't have to be in until later than that."

"What about your ride?" Mac asked.

"I'll tell them to come and get me later. I'd like to come ... you know, it *would* be some more hours. Quicker I do them the sooner I'm done."

He didn't answer right away. I didn't know if I should be happy or disappointed no matter what answer he gave.

"You make the call, just to make sure, and you can come with me. You know where the phone is."

"Yeah." I wandered out of the main part of the kitchen and into the little alcove that Mac had made into his home. It held his bed and a small TV and a few personal items sitting on top of his dresser. Unbelievably, this was his house and it wasn't nearly as big as our pool cabana. What would my parents think if they saw this? There was no worry there. They'd never see it. They'd never know and wouldn't care to know.

I picked up the phone—old, black, with a dial—like an antique. I dialed the number. It rang and rang and—

"Good evening, Blackburn residence."

"Hi, Berta, it's me."

"Hello, *Eon*."

That's how she always said my name—it wasn't *Ian,* it was *Eon*. I liked the way she said it.

"Can I speak to my mother or father?" I asked.

"They are both still out, Eon."

"Out? My mother knew I was going to be calling about now to get a ride home."

"She asked me to come and get you when you called. If you can give me directions I can—"

"I don't want a ride yet. It'll be a couple more hours, maybe three. I have more work to do."

"You can call when you're ready. I'm just here. I'll come for you."

"Thanks, Berta." I could always count on *her*.

"You be careful, *carino mio*."

"I will. Goodbye. I'll call later." I put the phone down.

Carino mio ... that was Spanish for "my dearest." That's what she called me all the time when I was little. Now she only said that to me when there was nobody around to hear. It still made me smile.

"It's all set," I said as I rejoined Mac.

He already had his jacket on and had a red backpack over his shoulder. I grabbed my coat off the peg behind the door.

"Let's get rolling," Mac said.

We left through the back door. It was chilly, especially after the misty, steamy warmth of the kitchen. The air smelled fresh—well, at least as fresh as air could be in the back alley in a big city. It was certainly better than the odours inside—that strange mixture of cooking and cleaning, sweat and grime, clothes that had been lived in, slept in and soiled.

Mac put a big padlock on the door and snapped it shut. He started walking but rather than heading up the alley toward the street, he followed the alley in the other direction ... away from the street lights.

"Cold tonight," Mac said and he gave a little shiver.

It was chilly.

"It's supposed to go down almost to freezing tonight," Mac said. "I always need to know what the temperature is going to be. A few degrees can mean the difference between life and death."

"How?" I asked.

"People who fall asleep outside can freeze to death."

"Do people really freeze to death in this city?" I asked skeptically.

"Every year one or two people. This year six."

"Come on ... really?"

"Really."

"It's just that I've never heard anything about it."

"Homeless people dying don't make the front page of the paper or the lead story on the evening news. It's always buried in the back ... the way they lead their lives. You remember saying you didn't believe how many homeless there are in the city?"

"Yeah," I said, feeling defensive.

"You're not seeing 'em because you're not looking for 'em. You have to spend time in the places you're not supposed to go ... places you'd be smart to stay away from ... places like the one we're going to go tonight."

We walked along in silence for a while.

"So tell me," Mac said, "how do you know Sarge?"

"I met him last night when I came down to do my volunteer hours," I said. "Met him in one of those places I'm probably not supposed to go. I was cutting across Selby Park and—"

"Selby Park! That wasn't very bright. It's not safe for you to be in there!"

"I didn't know that then. I know it now."

"Did something happen?" Mac asked.

I was tempted to leave some parts out—the parts that made me look stupid or weak—but if I'd done that there wouldn't have been any story to tell. I told him the whole thing.

"None of what you said surprises me," Mac said. "Especially the part about Sarge. If you've been around as long as I have, you get a pretty good handle on who can take care of themselves. Besides, he's a pretty big guy."

"You were going to tell me about him," I said.

"I'll tell you what I know and some of what I think I know and— Hey, how you doing?" Mac yelled out.

Two men were sitting on a heating grate behind a building. We were almost right on top of them but I hadn't seen them. They were hidden in the shadows and the steam that was rising out of the grate. There was an empty bottle on the ground beside them.

"You two doin' fine tonight?" Mac asked.

One of them mumbled out an answer. The other didn't respond. His eyes were open but I wasn't sure he was even aware of us standing over top of him.

"You two need a place to sleep tonight?" Mac asked. "The shelter still has space."

"No shelter," the man said. His words were slurred and thick. He was drunk or stoned or something. "We're okay ... leave us alone."

"Sure, we don't want to bother you, buddy. Here," Mac said. He handed the man some cigarettes. "Thought you could use these."

"Sure ... thanks ... you got a light?"

"'Course I do, buddy."

Mac pulled out a package of matches and the man, hands shaking, put the cigarette in his mouth. The match flared, throwing a little halo of light. As it came close to the cigarette—close to the man's face—I could make out his features. His eyes were dull and lifeless. His skin looked discoloured, like it was yellow. Maybe that was just the light from the match. He puffed on the cigarette and the end sparked to life.

"You need a meal tomorrow, you come by The Club, okay, buddy?" Mac said.

The man mumbled an answer I couldn't understand.

"See you later."

We started off down the alley.

"If I find somebody passed out and it's below freezing, I have to try and rouse 'em. Can't leave 'em there to freeze to death."

"What if you can't wake them or they wake up and tell you to leave them alone?" I asked.

"Either way I do the same. I call the police and ask them to come and pick them up. Better to be in jail than in a coffin."

"Have you ever found anybody who was … was …"

"Dead?"

I nodded.

He nodded back. "More than once. I've seen lots of things …" He shook his head slowly. "Maybe too many things."

We walked along in silence again. I felt uneasy, uncomfortable. Part of me wanted to know what he'd seen. A bigger part didn't want to hear. I needed to change the subject.

"You were starting to tell me about Sarge."

"I don't know a lot, but I'll tell you what I know. He's been on the streets—well, at least the streets around here—for about a year and a half. Before that I don't know for sure."

"But you said he was in the army … that's why they called him Sarge."

"That's what I heard."

"But you've never asked him?"

"You don't ever ask anybody anything about his past. You wait and if somebody talks, you listen."

"So you don't really know about him."

"I know it makes sense. The way you described him handling himself in the park, the way he carries himself."

"I noticed that," I said, cutting him off. "I just can't imagine how a guy in the army ends up on the street."

"Lots of people end up on the streets. Truck drivers, factory workers, businessmen, doctors."

"There are doctors living on the streets?" That couldn't be right.

"There's everybody."

"But why would a doctor end up on the streets?"

"Lots of routes to the same place, though there usually are two things that fuel the trip. Mental illness or substance abuse, usually alcohol. You've seen both already."

"But Sarge wasn't drunk and he's not crazy."

"I think they like the term 'mentally ill' better," Mac said.

"Okay, he doesn't seem mentally ill and he wasn't drunk."

"Not the two times you saw him," Mac said.

"There must be other reasons that people are on the streets."

Mac shook his head. "Not for the people I deal with. I'm not talking about kids. They hit the streets because of physical or sexual abuse, running away from a bad home situation, drug abuse, or some, a very few, just because of the thrill of being on their own. They think it's some sort of adventure. They find out pretty soon it ain't and most go back home, especially in the bad weather. In the summer the streets are filled with kids. The first good snowfall sends them all back home."

We came up to another group of men standing around a big garbage dumpster. All four of them greeted Mac enthusiastically.

"Looks a bit like rain tonight," Mac said, looking skyward. It was overcast.

"Hope not," one of them replied.

"Well, if it does, you know what you can do, eh?"

"Get wet," another answered and they all laughed.

"That or go into a shelter. Heaton House would still have space."

"They can keep their space."

As Mac talked to them, they passed a bottle from person to person. It was offered to Mac.

"Thanks but no thanks," Mac said politely.

"How about you?" the man asked, holding the bottle out to me.

I backed away, holding my hands up, shocked. I couldn't even imagine what diseases I could get sharing anything with this bunch.

"He's too young to drink," Mac said, answering for me.

"Never too young or too old."

Mac reached into his backpack and pulled out a package of cigarettes. "You boys want to split these?"

"Thanks, Mac."

"You're a real buddy."

We started off again.

"Do you give out cigarettes to everybody?" I asked.

"Best way to gain their trust and that's the best way to help them. Nobody accepts help from somebody they don't trust."

I guess that made sense. Besides, getting cancer wasn't what was going to kill these guys.

"If those men aren't going to a shelter, where will they sleep tonight?" I asked.

"I think they were standing right beside it."

"The building?"

"The dumpster," Mac said.

"They're going to sleep in a dumpster?"

"It gets them out of the wind. They can pull down the top for protection to keep dry if it rains. Not a bad place."

"But a dumpster ... how could they sleep with all that garbage?"

"There's garbage and then there's garbage. That dumpster is used by a furniture factory. The stuff they put in there, pieces of wood, bits of leather or plastic and foam, it makes a good place to sleep."

"But why wouldn't they just go to that place you mentioned … what was it?"

"Heaton House. It's a men's shelter. They can get a bed and a bath there."

"That doesn't sound bad. Why don't any of these guys want to go to a shelter?" I asked.

"Lots of people do use shelters, but just as many others don't."

We crossed a busy street and headed off into the dark of another back lane.

"Why wouldn't everybody go sleep in a shelter?" I asked.

"Lots of reasons. It can be crowded and loud and sometimes dangerous. There can be fights, people rippin' off your stuff. Some people can't stand being around people who're mentally ill. And some people just can't go. They're banned."

"Banned? What would somebody have to do to get banned?"

"Stealing, beating on people, or just being too crazy—"

"Don't you mean mentally ill?" I asked, chiding him.

"Nope. Crazy. Maybe being up all night screaming and yelling."

"Still, that has to be better than sleeping in a dumpster."

"There are some places that are better than both. Sometimes some of the boys get together, pool their money, and get a motel room or even a room that they can share for the winter. Sometimes they cobble together some boards and plastic and plywood and make a little shanty."

"A shanty?"

"A shack. There's a few of those down by the lake and more than a dozen under the freeway just over from here."

"And the police and the politicians let them do that?"

"As long as they stay in places where regular people don't see 'em then nobody bothers them. Others sleep under bridges, over top of sewer grates like those two guys we saw earlier, or in clothing drop boxes, doorways, telephone booths or bus shelters or—" He was counting on his fingers as he listed all the places.

"You can't be serious. You can't sleep in a telephone booth or a bus shelter," I said.

"You can sleep standing up if you're tired enough," Mac said. "Some have their own tents."

"Where would you pitch a tent?"

"Shelby Park, where you met Sarge. There's a spot in the middle where there's half a dozen tents. Come on, I'll show you."

"Should we be going there now?" I asked anxiously.

"It isn't a place *you* should ever be going by yourself, but if you're with me you're safe ... well, at least pretty safe." He paused. "You want me to drop you off instead?"

"No, I'll come with you," I said reluctantly. It wasn't that I didn't trust Mac but he was old, and not that big, and his baseball bat was back at the soup kitchen.

We came out of the back alleys and onto a street. The lights and traffic were reassuring. This wasn't my world, but at least it was familiar. As we walked we passed by more people—homeless people—moving along. It was like some sort of migration ... No, that wasn't right. A migration meant moving somewhere. These people were moving, but they were going nowhere.

The park was just up ahead. I felt increasingly uneasy. My anxiety increased as we entered, and my shoes crunched on the gravel path. This was certainly better than walking along the path without shoes. Would those three thugs be here in the park tonight, or would there be somebody even worse? If everybody on the street had a weapon, did Mac have one with him now? His baseball bat was a long ways away but maybe he had something else on him—a metal bar or a knife ... maybe a gun. I shook my head. Yeah, right, he had a gun ... maybe he had a bazooka up his sleeve.

Mac left the path and headed in through the bush. If going through the park wasn't safe, how much more dangerous was it to go off the path and into the forest? As Mac picked his way through the undergrowth, I tried to stay as close as possible. The ground was uneven and there were roots and stones sticking up. I moved as carefully as I could but in the darkness I kept stumbling and bumping into Mac.

"Do you know where you're going?" I asked.

"Does anybody really know where they're going?" he asked.

Great, just what I needed—a philosophy lesson.

"There's where we're going," Mac said. "Look."

Up ahead I caught glimmers of light flickering through the trees. It couldn't be ... it looked like—

"It's a fire."

We pushed through the last trees and found ourselves standing in a little clearing. In the opening were five tents and in the middle of the tents was a metal barrel, cut down low to the ground, holding a fire. Around the fire, sitting on lawn chairs, were eight or ten shadowy figures, their features lit up just a little by the flickering flames of the fire. This was unreal. We'd wandered out of the city, through a few trees, and into some sort of surreal campground. I half expected Yogi the bear to poke his head out of the trees and ask for a picnic basket!

"Mind if we join you gentlemen?" Mac asked.

A couple of men spun around to look in our direction. The others didn't seem to hear him.

"Come on over, always room for one or two more!" one of the men yelled out.

As we walked into the light of the campfire, I realized why the others hadn't responded. They were asleep—or more likely passed out—in their chairs.

Mac sat down on an empty stump and motioned for me to sit on the rock beside him. The fire was big enough to throw out heat and light. The warmth felt good.

The ground was littered with empty bottles. I tried to look at the bottles without being too obvious. Some of them were wine bottles— nothing fancy, and all with what appeared to be screw-top caps. There was also a bottle of cooking sherry. The other bottles had fallen label down and I couldn't tell what they were.

"Anybody seen Sarge tonight?" Mac asked.

"In there," one of the men said, gesturing to a green tent off to the side. "He turned in early."

That was why Mac had brought me here—this was where Sarge lived. I couldn't help but wonder if he'd gone to sleep or if he'd passed out like his buddies. I tried to figure out if any of these guys were at dinner tonight. It was hard to tell. In the dim, flickering light, buried underneath their toques and beards and dirt and layers of clothes they all looked pretty much the same to me. Maybe a couple of them had been at The Club tonight.

As Mac continued to talk, I felt a drop of moisture on my cheek. And then another and another. Great, it was starting to rain. A few degrees colder and snow would have been better.

"Mac … maybe we better get going—it's raining."

"We better. You guys might want to get inside too."

Seven

MAC WALKED ME to a fairly busy intersection. There were lots of cars and people ... regular people—couples walking hand in hand, and groups walking along the sidewalk, going to or from restaurants or the theatre or maybe the movies or shopping. We had travelled only about five blocks but we'd left behind one world and entered another—one much more familiar to me.

Mac had offered to stay and wait with me for my ride, but I told him to go on his way. He still had to finish his rounds. I'd used my cellphone to call home and I'd spoken to Berta. My parents still weren't home and she was on her way down to get me.

I watched the cars driving by. Half of them had bluish lights. Those were the type that expensive luxury cars like Mercedes, BMWs, Audis, and a dozen other types of prestige cars all had. It was amazing how many expensive cars there were—how many people had so much money to spend. And as I stood there watching and waiting I wondered—how many of those people driving in those expensive cars passed by the parks and alleys where the homeless were sitting or shuffling or sleeping, and never knew that there was anybody outside of the climate-controlled, leather-seated, CD surround sound that encircled them? How could some people have so much and others so little?

There was a gentle beep of a horn and a silver Mercedes rolled to a stop. It was Berta driving my mother's car. At night or on long trips she'd often drive my mother's car because her own car was so old that it wasn't particularly reliable. I grabbed the door and pulled it open, jumping inside without disturbing the flow of traffic too much. It was good to get into the car and out of the rain that had started falling more heavily. Wet and near freezing temperature was a bad combination.

"Hello, Eon."

"Thanks for coming to get me," I said as I snapped on my seatbelt. Berta pulled away.

"I'm sorry to make you come out so late. I thought my parents would be home by now."

"They got home just before I left. I offered to go because they looked … they looked … tired."

Tired. That meant they'd both probably been drinking. I doubted that it involved anything with a screw top.

"Did you have a good evening?" Berta asked.

"I don't know if 'good' is the right word." We were passing Selby Park. "You see that park there," I said, pointing to the scene rolling by outside the passenger window. "There are people who live in there."

Berta nodded but didn't answer.

"Really. I'm serious. They have tents and chairs and there's a bunch of them sitting around a fire right now."

"And how do *you* know that?" she asked.

That was stupid. I shouldn't have said anything. "Is this just between me and you?" I asked.

"If that is what you want, Eon."

I knew I could trust Berta. "I was with Mac, the man who runs the soup kitchen. I went with him on one of the walks he does every night to look out for people who are living on the streets. Mac told me there are thousands and thousands living on the streets," I explained.

Berta shook her head in disbelief. "Thousands ... so hard to believe. I only see a few."

"That's what *I* said! Tonight I saw them, where they live in alleys and dumpsters and parks."

"These are not good places for you to go," Berta said. "Maybe it is better that your mother doesn't know about these things."

"I'm not telling her. She probably wouldn't believe it even if I did tell her."

"She might believe. There are homeless everywhere. That is how it is in Guatemala."

The park disappeared from view.

"I hadn't really thought about that. Are there many?"

"Many thousands."

"I didn't know that. I figured it was just like Mexico and there weren't many street people."

Berta laughed. "They do not have beggars in the fancy resorts where you and your family stayed. They are hidden like here. The same way."

"At least in Guatemala they don't have to worry about freezing to death like they do here."

"Freezing to death is not what they fear."

"What do they fear?"

Berta didn't answer. She stared straight ahead out the windshield, the wipers moving silently across the glass to clear away the rain that had gotten even harder.

"Berta ... what do they have to fear?"

She still didn't answer right away and I thought she wasn't going to when she started. "In my country people on the street die all the time."

"I guess even in a warm country you can still starve to death."

"They do not starve. They are killed. Dozens and dozens. Maybe hundreds. Maybe more. They are gunned down."

I could scarcely believe what she was saying. "Can't the police or the army protect them?"

"The police and army," Berta sneered. "Who do you think does the killing?"

"That can't be right."

"Right it is not. True it is. I ... I should not be telling of these things. Not now. Not yet."

"Why not?"

"It is too soon."

"I'm almost sixteen, Berta. I can handle it."

"It is not that it is too soon for you, Eon. It is too soon for *me*."

Eight

"IAN!"

I turned around. It was Robert. He moved around the crush of kids streaming through the corridor toward classes.

"So why weren't you there Friday night?" Robert asked.

"Why wasn't I where?" I asked.

"Jen's party."

"I forgot all about it," I said.

"You missed a good party. Lots of food, some beer, lots of ladies."

"So where were you?" Justin asked.

"Community service hours for civics."

"On a Friday night?" he asked in disbelief.

"Like I have a choice. I have to put in the hours. No choice."

"Too bad. A couple of the girls were even asking about you."

"Anyone in particular?" I asked.

"The usual suspects."

The bell rang, loud, echoing through the hall and setting off a wave of activity as lockers slammed and kids hurried to class.

"See you at lunch," Robert said.

"Sure. See you."

I had completely forgotten about that party and I had been looking forward to it.

We filed into class. I just hoped I could get my usual seat at the back of the room.

"Ian?" Mrs. Watkins asked.

I stopped. Instinctively I wondered just what it was that I'd done wrong, or failed to read, or hadn't handed in. But really there was nothing ... at least nothing that I could remember.

"So, did you go back to your placement this weekend?" she asked.

I stopped by her desk. "I was there on Friday night. I put in six hours."

"In one night?" She sounded surprised or like she was doubting me.

"It was a long night. There are lots of people to feed and lots of work to do. I'm going back tonight."

"I'm impressed."

"Impressed or surprised?" I asked.

She gave a little smirk. "Both. You think you could tell your class-mates about your placement at the end of class today?"

"I could ... I guess."

"Excellent."

I turned to walk away. By now all the seats in the back of the class were taken. I did a quick scan of the room. The only open seats were in the front row. I took the one farthest off to the side.

"Now as you recall," Mrs. Watkins began, "from our last class, we learned that, contrary to what some people may have thought, Lester Pearson was not a left winger for the Toronto Maple Leafs. We learned that he was a Canadian prime minister who received the Nobel Prize in 1957. Does anybody remember what Nobel Prize he received?"

There was no answer. It wasn't that I didn't know, or that lots of people didn't remember, it was just that we didn't necessarily volunteer what we knew.

"Surely somebody must remember?" she prodded.

"Best supporting actor?" a voice chipped in from the back to accompanying laughter.

"How about if I give everybody an additional assignment if somebody doesn't give me the right answer," Mrs. Watkins said.

"Peace, he got it for peace!" a voice yelled out.

"Right. It's good to know that I'm not *completely* wasting my breath when I talk. This Nobel Peace Prize was awarded to Lester Pearson because of his pivotal role in the conception and creation of the United Nations Peacekeeping Force. Since 1956 there have been peacekeeping missions throughout the world. These missions have been in Europe, the Middle East, Africa, Asia, Central and South America. Does anybody know exactly what roles are played by peacekeepers?"

"Keeping the peace would be my guess, Mrs. Watkins," Kelsey said.

She shook her head slowly as the chuckling died down. "The roles of the peacekeeper can vary tremendously. Peacekeepers can be used to disarm warring factions, to protect or repatriate refugees," she said, tapping her pencil on the desk as she recited the list, "ensure human rights, supervise governments or elections of governments, train or supervise local police forces, ensure the distribution of relief supplies, and most often, stand as a thin *blue* line between sides that are, or *were,* at war." She paused. "Why did I say blue line? And before anybody can give a smart-ass answer it has nothing to do with hockey."

"Because that's the colour of their helmets, berets, and vehicles," said a girl sitting just behind me.

"Obviously at least one person has done their reading," Mrs. Watkins said, trying to look stern. "Since most armed forces try to avoid being seen, their uniforms and vehicles are in browns or greens or sand colours, depending on the region where the conflict is taking place. Rather than trying to blend in, the UN peacekeepers want to be seen. By being seen it is hoped that they can avoid being mistaken as a combatant." Mrs. Watkins took a sip from the coffee sitting on her desk. "Since 1956 Canada has had over a hundred thousand members of our armed forces in these missions. We have contributed more soldiers to more missions than any other country. That is why we are known around the world as a peace-loving country."

"Obviously nobody's been watching us play hockey," somebody added.

"Obviously not," Mrs. Watkins agreed. "But there is a cost. Peacekeeping missions, although sanctioned by the United Nations, are primarily paid for by the countries that supply the soldiers. There is also another cost." She paused. "Being dressed in a blue helmet or driving in a blue vehicle doesn't make you bulletproof. Since its inception there have been over eighteen hundred deaths of United Nations peacekeepers."

There was a gasp from the class, but not from me. I knew the number because I'd done the reading on Sunday. I'd actually found it pretty interesting.

"This number seems large, but remember that there have been hundreds and hundreds of thousands of soldiers from countries around the world that have been posted in these missions. Does anybody know which country has suffered the most fatalities?"

"India," I said quietly.

"That's right, Ian," she said, spinning around to face me. I didn't think she would have heard me. "They have suffered one hundred and nine deaths. Ian, do you know which country has had the second-most deaths?"

"Canada. One hundred and seven … and counting."

She nodded. "And counting. As we speak, there are Canadians serving in missions in the former Yugoslavia, Africa and Central America, the Middle East and Asia. For a relatively small armed forces—we have approximately sixty thousand men and women in uniform—we stretch ourselves around the globe." Mrs. Watkins took another sip from her coffee. "Just out of curiosity, does anybody here have a member of their family who is in the armed forces?"

There was no response.

"Does anybody even *know* anybody who is in the military?"

Again no answer.

"Surely *somebody* must know *somebody* who *was* in the military."

"I do," I said. "Sort of."

"He was sort of in the military or you sort of know him?" Mrs. Watkins asked.

"I sort of know him."

"Is this somebody you've talked to recently?"

"This past week."

"And will you be talking to him in the near future?" she asked.

"Probably … I could … I guess."

"In that case I have an assignment for you, Ian."

I cringed. Why hadn't I kept my mouth shut instead of showing off?

"Actually it's an assignment for Ian or anybody else who would like to earn some bonus marks."

"So this is a voluntary assignment?" somebody asked.

"Completely," she said. "Although there are some people who could clearly use the bonus marks if they hope to make grade ten civics a one-year project."

She wasn't looking at me but I knew she was talking to me.

"The assignment is to interview a member of the armed forces. To ask him, or her, about where they were assigned, to discover if they were part of a United Nations–sanctioned peace mission, to get their opinions, to hear of their experiences. That is the assignment. Any questions?"

The only question I had was whether I could afford to risk not doing this assignment. I didn't think that was an option.

"Before we go any further discussing our reading, I'd like to take this opportunity to have Ian tell us about his community service placement," Mrs. Watkins said.

Great, I'd thought she'd forgotten about me. I slowly got to my feet and turned around so I was facing the class. I guess that was one good thing about sitting in the front—although if I'd been in the back, and kept my mouth shut, she probably wouldn't have remembered I was even there.

"If I'm not mistaken, Ian is the last person in the class to report on his placement. Is there anybody else?" she asked.

Nobody answered. I just stood there, on display—the poster boy for being the last. Was she trying to make me look stupid?

"Please begin, Ian."

"Sure. I'm volunteering at a place called the Club. It's a place that feeds street people."

"Do they, like, give out sandwiches or something?" a girl asked.

"No, it serves meals, real meals ... beef stew and spaghetti ... things like that. It's good food."

"Sounds like you've tried the food," Mrs. Watkins commented.

"I know what it looks and smells like and the people really seem to like it," I said. I didn't want anybody to know that I'd eaten there. "I help serve the food and clean up afterwards."

"So you're like the cafeteria ladies," a guy at the back—Jason—said and then chuckled. I'd known him since grade five. I hadn't liked him since grade five.

"Do you have to wear a hairnet too?" Chris, his friend, said.

There were a couple more muffled chuckles. I crossed my arms over my chest and stared at the two guys—the two *jerks*. I looked at one and then the other and then focused on the first, locking eyes. I stared Jason down until he dropped his eyes to the desk. Jerk. Wimpy jerk. Maybe out there on the downtown streets I wasn't tough, but here was a different thing.

"People who've never been there might be tempted to make *stupid* comments," I said, my eyes still on the two guys, daring them to say something, even let a smirk cross their faces. Neither did.

"It's not just about serving food, it's about saving lives. These people would die if it wasn't for programs like this one."

"It sounds like you're really making a difference," Mrs. Watkins said.

"Not me," I protested. "I just show up and help out a little. The guy who makes it work is Mac. He lives there."

"It's not uncommon for people running these sorts of places to spend an enormous amount of hours at their work so it seems like they practically live there," Mrs. Watkins said.

"No, you don't understand … he really *does* live there … in the back. But it also is his life."

"It sounds like you admire what he does."

"I guess I do," I admitted, although I'd never really thought about it until this conversation.

I had been confused by what Mac did, by his dedication, although I also gave him credit. Whether you believed it was something admirable or not, you had to admit that he was prepared to back his beliefs with his actions. He walked the walk. He reminded me of Berta that way. She was always doing something for her church or driving people to things like hospital appointments, and I didn't even want to guess how much money she'd sent back to support foster children in Guatemala.

"Do you think that this gentleman would be willing to come to our class and speak sometime?" Mrs. Watkins asked.

I burst out laughing before I pulled the laughter back inside. "He's pretty busy." Way too busy to waste his time talking to a bunch of kids in some stupid civics class, I thought but didn't say.

"He sounds really dedicated," Mrs. Watkins said approvingly. She turned to the class. "I was wondering, when people think of street people, what comes to mind? Give me one word, just throw them out. One word."

"Homeless," Kelsey said.

"Definitely homeless or they wouldn't be on the street. What else?"

"Drunks."

"Drug addicts," Justin said.

"Runaways."

"No," I said. "Not the people we're feeding. These aren't kids. These are men, almost all men, older men. Some are really, really old."

"Other words?" Mrs. Watkins asked.

"Bums."

"Hobos."

"Crazy as a loon," one of the two jokers at the back said.

"The term is mentally ill," I said. I wasn't finding either of them particularly funny today or any other day.

"Calling people crazy or loony, or saying they're a few bricks short of a load, or are a nut, is all part of a dangerous process," Mrs. Watkins said. "If somebody is a nut, then they are no longer a person, and if they are not a person, then you can treat them as *less*. That dehumanizing process allows people to feel it is acceptable to treat them badly." Mrs. Watkins took another sip from her coffee. "Any other words?"

"Worthless," a girl, Heather, said.

Nobody said anything. The word just hung there and everybody just stared at it. I knew this girl. She was smart and nice. She hadn't said it to be mean or a smartass.

"Ian?" Mrs. Watkins said. "Are these street people worthless?"

I shook my head slowly. "Nobody is worthless."

"I guess the real question isn't are they worthless, but are they worth *less* … less than other people."

Nobody volunteered an answer.

"Ian?"

I knew what the correct answer was, what I was expected to say—that they were worth just as much as anybody else.

"Well?"

"I'm supposed to say that everybody is worth the same," I said. "But that's not the way we treat them."

"How do we treat them?" Mrs. Watkins asked.

"We treat them like they're worth practically nothing, so maybe that's what society really does think of them," I said.

The bell rang, startling me so much that I flinched.

"On that note, class dismissed."

People started getting up and gathering their books and belongings.

"And I expect those who didn't complete the previous reading to complete it before starting on the next two chapters ... all to be done by tomorrow. Expect a *surprise* test!" Mrs. Watkins yelled out over the noise of the crowd.

There was a chorus of groans and boos and comments.

Mrs. Watkins turned to me. "And, Ian, can you please stay behind for a few seconds?"

Was this becoming a trend? I went over to her desk and waited as everybody shuffled out of the class.

"Ian, are you going to interview that member of the armed forces?" she asked.

"I'm going to try."

"Good. You could use the marks." She paused. "Ian, do you ever wonder why I'm so hard on you?"

I shrugged. "I just thought you were hard on everybody."

She laughed. "I am, just more on some people. People I think have potential but aren't using it. People like you," she said, tapping a finger against my chest.

"Me?"

"Don't try to sound so surprised. You know better than anybody else that you hardly ever give it your best effort. Although it does seem like an awful lot of work to act so uninterested, detached, and bored all the time. Wouldn't it be easier to just do the work instead of trying to figure out a way around it?"

"I'm going to try to interview that soldier," I protested.

"Don't try to do it. Do it. See you tomorrow."

Nine

"You want some more juice?" I asked one of the men.

He held his plastic cup up in answer. I poured, trying to keep the flow of juice in the middle of the cup that was violently shaking in his hand. I stopped when it was half filled—I didn't want it to get too full. Less to clean up if he spilled it.

It was different being out here among the men, walking between the tables, instead of serving the food from behind the counter. The counter job was being filled tonight by three middle-aged, friendly, smiling lady volunteers. All three of them had big hair, bright-coloured dresses, and buttons that read *Jesus Saves*. Apparently, judging from the jewellery they were all wearing, Jesus had been saving up for diamonds and fancy earrings. How stupid, wearing things like that down here ... even more stupid than wearing fancy running shoes.

Mac had made no secret to me of what he thought of those volunteer ladies and their Jesus buttons. He hated people like that— those do-gooders. He also said regardless of what he thought, he did welcome their helping hands and the money that might flow from their church.

I could have seen Berta working here, helping out. Part of me thought that would have been cool, to work beside her. The bigger part of me didn't want her anywhere near this place. She wasn't equipped to deal with this sort of situation. Berta was just too gentle and kind and I would have had to spend all my time watching out for her. I wondered if that was how Mac felt about me ... not the gentle and kind part, but having to watch out for me.

I scanned the room until I found Mac. He was standing just off to the side, watching. I wasn't sure if he was there to protect the church ladies from the men or the men from the church ladies. Probably both.

With them serving, my job was to clean off the tables, top up the drinks, and even hand out some extra buns and apples that had been donated and would go stale and bad if they weren't eaten soon. At first I'd been nervous doing the new job. It was different. More exposed. And that made it seem more dangerous. At least that's the way it felt. Serving food had kept me a countertop removed from everybody, and while holding a serving spoon or spaghetti tongs wasn't like having a gun in my hands it somehow seemed better than simply having a pitcher of juice to defend myself.

As I walked around I was completely ignored by some of the men, while others were friendly and polite. One guy acted like he knew me—like we were long-lost friends. That was particularly strange since I *knew* that I'd never seen him before.

I was keeping one eye open for Sarge to arrive. So far no sign, but he'd come late the last time as well. Mac had told me that there were times when Sarge was here every night for weeks at a time. Then he wouldn't show up for even longer. I just hoped this wasn't the start of one of those disappearing acts. It was okay if he didn't show up tonight, or even for a few days, but longer than that wouldn't work.

I'd started to wonder if I could get away with faking an interview. Who would know if I just pretended I talked to him? No ... Mrs. Watkins was pretty smart and she'd see right through it. I really needed to interview him. I needed the marks. Strange ... I also didn't want to disappoint Mrs. Watkins. I had no idea where that came from.

I picked up the tray that I'd loaded with dirty dishes. The weight caught me off guard and for a second I thought I was going to drop it. That wouldn't have been the same tragedy as dropping my mother's expensive imported dishes but it still wouldn't have been good.

Mac was already in the kitchen when I pushed through the door. He was standing at the sink and he had started to do the dishes.

"First I don't get to serve food and now I don't get to wash up. You trying to replace me?" I joked.

"Nope. Like you so much I'm thinking of doubling your salary. Wait ... two times nothin' is still nothin', right?"

"I think so."

"In that case, let's triple it!"

"Thanks for the vote of confidence." I set the tray down on the counter.

"You're pretty good with the guys," Mac said. "You seem to know how to talk to them ... and when it's better to just shut up."

"I've had years of experience learning when to shut up," I said. "Although I'd much rather be talking to somebody tonight." I'd told Mac about the assignment. I wasn't sure he approved of it, but he didn't tell me not to do it.

"Looks like Sarge is a no-show. If I see him around, you want me to tell him you want to talk?" Mac asked.

"I'd appreciate that."

"'Course there's no guarantee that he'll talk to you," Mac warned.

"I just want to ask him a few questions."

"Askin' don't mean you get any answers."

"I'm not asking anything too personal, just stuff about being in the military."

Mac shook his head. "No tellin' what's personal and what's not. No tellin' what put somebody on the streets. You just be careful about what you ask, okay?"

"I'll try. That's if I even get to see him."

"Don't you worry. I always find that people, and things, turn up when you most need them."

"Now you sound like some sort of minister again. I hope you're right."

I took the last of the dishes off the tray and stacked them on the counter, ready to be washed.

"I'll go back for another load."

I'd no sooner pushed through the door into the dining area than I saw him—Sarge! He was standing there in line waiting to be served. I put down the tray and picked up a serving spoon, inserting myself between two of the church ladies who were giving out the food.

"I'm going to help for a while," I said. "That will speed things up a little." That wasn't a complete lie. It would make the line move faster. The real reason of course was that I wanted an excuse to start talking to him. Besides, if I gave him food he might be more willing to talk to me and answer my questions. It would be sort of an unofficial, unspoken trade.

Tonight's meal was chicken stew. It was thick, filled with potatoes and vegetables. It smelled really good. If there was any left at the end of the night I'd find out if it tasted as good as it smelled.

"Hi, how you doing?" I asked.

He looked up. "I'm doing well, Ian. And you?"

"Good." I took a deep breath. "I was sort of wondering if when you're through eating I could ask you a few questions."

"Questions about what?" he asked suspiciously.

"Nothing too personal ... just a few questions ... it's for a school assignment."

"I'm not sure if I'm able to help with much to do with school, but we could talk. You come over when you're able to get free."

"Thanks." I gave him two extra big spoons of stew. I wanted to make sure he'd be eating for as long as possible.

I couldn't very well run off right away—although I wanted to. I continued to serve the next half-dozen people in line. As I kept serving I had one eye on the bowls and the other on Sarge. He walked over to the far corner and took a seat at a nearly empty table. He had his back to the wall, the way he'd sat before. He sat silently, eyes on his meal, eating. Lots of people focused only on their food, but I got the feeling he was lost in thought.

"There, I think we're caught up," I said to one of the church ladies. All three nodded their heads and smiled sweetly at me. They certainly were friendly. I put down my serving spoon.

I suddenly felt anxious. What exactly was I going to say? What was I going to ask? Besides, Mac had warned me, more than once, about asking anybody too many questions. What was it he had said—that he listened but didn't ask. Sarge looked up from his meal, saw me, smiled, and waved. I felt better.

I sat down on the bench across from him.

"You're not going to eat?" he asked.

"I'll eat later ... if there's any left."

"Now I feel badly," he said. "I shouldn't have taken so much."

"No, that's okay!" I exclaimed. "I can always eat later when I get home."

"So, what did you want to talk about?" he asked. I couldn't help noticing that he smelled like alcohol. I'd never noticed that before. "Is it about being homeless?"

"No. It's about being in the armed forces."

"Why would you want to talk to me about that?" he asked.

"Well, I thought ... Mac told me ... that he thought you used to be in the military," I stammered, now feeling embarrassed.

"Why would he think that?"

"I guess because of what people call you sometimes."

"Sarge?" he said.

"I thought ... *Mac* thought ... that because they call you Sarge you were in the military, and I have to try to interview somebody who was in the army. I'm sorry for bothering you." Feeling flustered I started to get up, but he put a hand on my arm, holding me in place.

"You can interview me," he said. "I was in the military."

"You were a sergeant?"

He nodded his head. "Special ops ... I was trained in many things, including unarmed combat."

"That's why you were able to take on those thugs so easily."

"Technically I wasn't unarmed ... I had an iron bar ... but that's the idea behind the training."

"I'd love to be able to do things like that, to be able to take care of myself," I said.

"If you're smart you just stay away from places where you might need those skills. Either that or join the army and get the training."

I laughed.

"You think joining the army is funny?" he asked.

"No, of course not!" I exclaimed. "I just never thought of it, that's all."

"Maybe you should."

This led straight into one of my questions. "Would you recommend the armed forces as a job for somebody to pursue?"

He thought for a moment. "I think there's a need for people to become part of the military. It is a career that involves honour ... a job where you can help people."

I got slightly out of my seat so I could pull a pen and piece of paper out of my back pocket. I unfolded the paper and flattened it out so I could read the rest of my questions.

"How long were you in the military?"

"Almost twenty-four years."

"Wow, that's a long time!"

"It didn't seem like it. One day I'm in military college and the next day I'm sitting here talking to you. The time just went."

I looked at the next question. "Why did you decide to join the military?"

"I always knew what I was going to become. My father was in the military, and his father before him. I grew up on army bases."

I scribbled down his answer.

"People often choose the same career as their parents. What does your father do?" he asked.

"He's a businessman," I said. He was more than just a businessman. He was the CEO of one of the biggest companies in the city. I just didn't want to mention that.

"Then perhaps you'll become a businessman too."

"Maybe," I said, although I doubted it. I didn't know what I wanted to be but I was certain I wasn't following in the footsteps of either parent.

"Wouldn't be a bad job," he said. "At least you could spend time with your family."

Obviously he didn't know much about businessmen—or at least my father's style of being a businessman. I felt myself getting angry inside as I thought about my father always being at work. He really didn't have to be gone so often—he could spend more time with us if he wanted. The angry feelings surprised me. Usually it just didn't bother me any more.

"Me being gone on assignment in far-flung foreign countries was hard on my wife," he said.

"I didn't know you had a wife."

"I did ... I guess I still do."

I didn't know what to say to any of that. I felt embarrassed and sad and terrible for even bringing it up at all. I looked down at my paper.

"You know, when I decided to enlist, my father said something to me, something I will never forget. He said that I must go into this not expecting ever to be thanked. Not by the government, or civilians, and not even by the army itself. No one would ever recognize the nature of the sacrifices that I would make," he said.

I scribbled down his answer, not even understanding it and not knowing if what he was saying made any sense.

"You said you were stationed in different places. Where?" I asked.

"We lived in bases across the country from one coast to the other, both when I was growing up and then when I enlisted myself. It's hard to move, leave behind friends, but it's the way of the military."

"We're studying Canada's role as peacekeepers. Were you ever part of any peacekeeping missions?"

"I was," he said. "I proudly wore the blue beret of the United Nations. It was a sacrifice for me, but more for my wife. I would be gone for three or six months or even longer."

"That would be hard."

"My wife had to make do without a husband for months on end. And of course there is always the worry ... worry about something happening."

"I was surprised by how many soldiers have been killed in peace-keeping missions," I said.

He gave me a questioning look.

"I've been reading about it for my civics course. Canada has had over a hundred deaths," I explained.

"And many more people injured or maimed for life. Legs blown off by land mines don't grow back." He paused. "You've read about it. I've lived it. Seen the deaths, seen the injuries. People I served with, people who were my friends. But that is to be expected. A soldier must be willing to sacrifice his life for his country in times of war and there is a very thin line between peacekeeping and war ... a very thin line."

"Where were you stationed?" I asked.

"It seems like everywhere. Six months in Bosnia after the fall of Yugoslavia, Haiti, the Middle East on two missions, and finally in Rwanda."

"Rwanda ... in Africa," I said, but I wasn't completely certain if it was there or in South America.

"Central Africa, the Great Lakes Region." He slowly shook his head. "What a tragedy, what a great tragedy."

"What was a tragedy?" I asked, wondering if a friend was killed there.

He looked up from his meal. He looked shocked ... no, angry ... no, hurt. "You don't know?"

"Sorry."

"You know nothing about it ... nothing about what happened there, do you?"

I shook my head.

He didn't answer. Slowly he pushed his plate—still half full—away from him. "I don't want to talk any more." He rose to his feet and walked away.

I sat there dumbfounded, not knowing what to say or think or do. I just watched him walk out the door.

Ten

I GOT UP and stumbled away, back toward the kitchen.

"What happened?" Mac asked from behind the counter. He was holding a tray of dirty dishes. Obviously he'd seen Sarge walk out.

"I don't know."

I walked into the kitchen and Mac trailed behind me.

"What did you say to him?" Mac asked.

"I didn't say anything ... well, not much."

"You must have said something."

"He was upset because I didn't know about Rwanda."

"Wanda? Wanda who?"

"Not *Wanda*. *Rwanda*. The country."

"Oh, yeah, sure, I've heard of it, it's in Africa."

"He was upset because I didn't know what happened there," I explained. "He said there was a tragedy ... a *great* tragedy that happened."

Mac shrugged. "Always one tragedy or another in Africa." He set the tray down.

"But do you know what he was talking about ... specifically?" I asked.

"No idea."

"That wasn't fair that he got mad at me for not knowing something that *you* didn't even know about," I complained.

"Bad example. I only know what happens around here. I don't watch the news, except to get the weather, and I only read the comics and sports sections in the papers," Mac said. "If I want tragedy I don't have to look to Africa. All I gotta do is look outside my door."

WHEN I GOT HOME I went straight up to my room and looked in my backpack, grabbing my geography textbook. I jumped onto my bed and opened the book. I went straight to the back, to the index, flipped through, and scanned down until I found Rwanda listed—pages 159 to 161. I flipped back to the listed pages.

At the top of the first page was a flag—I guess the Rwandan flag. A band of sky blue across the top with a sun in the corner and then a band of yellow and the bottom third green. It was sort of a pretty flag, but awfully simple. It didn't look like a real flag, but more like something some kid in grade five had made up for a social studies project.

Below that was a map. It was a tiny little piece of land, so small that the name "Rwanda" had to be spelled in smaller letters than the neighbouring countries. It was dead centre in the middle of Africa— it was landlocked with neighbours on all sides and no ocean. I remembered enough from my grade nine geography to know that no coasts meant limited trade and limited money.

One border was shared with Tanzania. Burundi was at the bottom. The Congo on the other side and Uganda on the top. I'd heard of the last two, although I didn't know anything about them. There were a couple of fairly big lakes, some rivers marked on the map, and I assumed since it had a star that the capital city of Rwanda was someplace named Kigali.

It certainly didn't look very big. I scanned down the page to a section marked *FACTS*.

Total land area: 26,338 square kilometres.

That was tiny. From what I could remember that was much smaller than Lake Ontario. The entire country could be slipped into Lake Ontario and still have space to spare. No wonder nobody had ever heard of it.

Natural resources: tin ore, tungsten, methane, hydropower generation.

I guess that would be from all those rivers—and arable land.

Population: 7,810,000.

What? That wasn't possible. How could that many people live in that little a country? I read the text. It said that number was an estimate ... there had never been a census ... and that there was a high rate of mortality due to AIDS, higher infant mortality rate, and a generally high death rate.

Official languages: French, English and Kinyarwanda.

Kinyarwanda ... I'd never heard of it. It was probably something they only spoke in Rwanda. At least if the people knew English they could get movies and TV shows and ... did they even have TV? They had to. No country was so backward that they didn't get MTV.

I kept scanning the facts. *The country is a republic ... independent since 1962 ... former colony of Belgium ... population in rural areas ... most densely populated country in Africa*—no kidding—*few natural resources ... big foreign debt ... 60% of population below the poverty line ... 90% of labour force in agriculture ... average life expectancy, 39.33 years*—

People had to live twice as long here. I shook my head.

In a nutshell, it was a poor, rural country with too many people, not enough resources, more than half the people lived in poverty, the whole *country* itself was poor, AIDS was rampant, babies died too often and everybody else died young. Why would the United Nations even be in this place? It wasn't like it had enough of anything that anybody was going to bother fighting over.

Now that I knew more about the country I had to know about what had happened there and it certainly wasn't in my book. How big a tragedy could it be if it didn't even rate a mention? Then again, this was a geography book, so unless the tragedy involved a volcanic eruption it probably wouldn't have been written about.

I climbed off my bed and flopped down on the chair in front of the computer. I wiggled the mouse and the screen came to life. I went to Google and keyed in a search.

Rwanda ... no, that wouldn't work, that would just give me more about the country. I needed to know what had happened when Sarge was there as a peacekeeper—that was it. I backspaced out "Rwanda" and typed in "United Nations Peacekeeping" and hit Enter. The search engine came up with more than twenty-four thousand sites. I clicked on the first and a site popped up.

It had the UN logo in the top, sky blue background, like the colour on the Rwandan flag, like I imagined the blue berets of the peace-keepers would be. In big letters it read, "Peacekeeping ... in the service of peace," and below that it listed the parts of the world where they had, or still had, missions. I highlighted Africa—at least I knew that much—but there were no current operations. I went to past operations and did the same. There was Rwanda, along with a strange heading: UNAMIR. I clicked on the site.

The United Nations Assistance Mission for Rwanda (UNAMIR) was in operation from October 1993 to March 1996. It was originally established to help implement the Arusha Peace Agreement signed by warring Rwandese parties on August 4, 1993. The mandate and strength of this mission were adjusted on a number of occasions in response to the tragic events and the changing situation within the country.

Tragic events ... what tragic events? I clicked over to the facts-and-figures button. There, under force commanders were listed two Canadians—Major-General Roméo A. Dallaire (October 1993–August 1994), and Major-General Guy Tousignant (August 1994–December 1995). Obviously there were Canadians who had participated in Rwanda. Under that it listed the countries involved. I counted forty different countries and the total strength, ranging from around a thousand personnel up to over five thousand. At the bottom, the last line listed fatalities: 3 military observers, 22 other military personnel, 1 civilian police and 1 local staff—27 in total. People had died. Had he seen somebody die, a good friend, somebody he was in the military with, and that's why he got so upset? Was that the tragedy? I needed to know more. I clicked on the summary section of the page.

Fighting between the mainly Hutu government of Rwanda and the Tutsi-led Rwandese Patriotic Front (RPF) broke out in October 1990. A number of ceasefire agreements were negoti-ated, culminating in the Arusha agreement signed on July 22, 1992. As a term of the ongoing negotiations to establish power

sharing between the two parties there was created a 50-member
Neutral Military Observer Group furnished by the Organization
of African Unity (OAU). Hostilities recommenced in February
1993, interrupting the negotiations and a request was made for
United Nations involvement. The Arusha talks, brokered by
Tanzania and the OAU, reconvened and led to the signing of a
comprehensive peace accord in August 1993. This accord called
for a democratically elected government and provided for the
establishment of a broad-based transitional government until
the elections, repatriation of refugees and the integration of the
armed forces of the two sides. Both sides asked the United
Nations to assist in the implementation of this agreement. In
October 1993 resolution 872 established the creation of an
international force, the United Nations Assistance Mission for
Rwanda (UNAMIR). This force was mandated to help implement the agreement, monitor its implementation and support
the transitional government. This force, initially composed of a
battalion strength force—400 from Belgium and 400 from
Bangladesh—under the Command of Major-General Roméo
Dallaire (Canada) was established on December 24, 1993. It took
an additional five months for the force to reach its authorized
strength of 2,548. In addition many unresolved issues between
the parties delayed implementation and the transitional government was never inaugurated.

In April 1994 the Presidents of Rwanda and Burundi were
killed while returning from ongoing peace talks in Tanzania.
These deaths set off an unprecedented wave of political and
ethnic killings that included the slaying of the Prime Minister of
Rwanda, cabinet ministers and UNAMIR peacekeepers. The
killings, primarily targeting Tutsi and moderate Hutus, were
carried out by the Rwanda armed forces, the presidential guard,

and militia. It is estimated that in the 100-day period subsequent to the plane crash a genocide ensued that resulted in the massacre of 800,000 people.

Eight hundred thousand people—that couldn't be right. That must be a typo ... maybe somebody had put in an extra zero or two. There was no way that that many people could have been killed. I'd have heard about something that big.

By October 1994 estimates suggest that out of a population of 7.9 million, close to 800,000 people had been killed, 2,000,000 had fled to neighbouring countries and an additional 2,000,000 persons had been internally displaced. A Commission established by the Security Council of the United Nations reported that there was "overwhelming evidence" that proved that Hutu elements had committed acts of genocide against the Tutsi people in a "concerted, planned, systematic, and methodical way."

Genocide. I knew that word. It was like the Holocaust ... World War II ... what Hitler and the Nazis had done to the Jews. Genocide wasn't about soldiers killing soldiers—that was bad enough, but that's what happened in wars, what the soldiers expected to happen. In a genocide it was just regular people being killed—slaughtered—because of who they were. The Nazis targeted Jews. Men, women, children, old people, babies. They were killed because they were Jews. How many had been killed? Was it six million ... eight million ... I couldn't remember exactly, but I knew it was mind-boggling, not believable.

At least I knew something about the Holocaust. We'd taken it in history classes and I'd watched war movies on TV, and my grandfather had even been in that war. Why didn't I know anything about Rwanda? No wonder Sarge had been so angry and upset. He'd been there, been part of that insanity, that tragedy, and I didn't even know anything about it. Nothing. How was that even possible?

Eleven

"I really appreciate you driving me," I said to Berta.

"That is fine," she answered. "But I'm still not sure ... why are you going downtown on a school day instead of to *school*? Shouldn't you be going to school?"

"I'm doing this *for* school," I said. I always found that part of the truth was the best lie. Nobody, including Mrs. Watkins, would have approved of me skipping school to complete the interview. "I'm interviewing somebody for an assignment."

"And who is this somebody? The man where you are working? You could interview him any time you are down there, yes?"

"I could, but it's not Mac I'm interviewing. It's a soldier ... a former soldier. It's for bonus marks in civics."

"Bonus marks would be good. It would make your mama and papa happy." She gave me a big smile.

"I'm not doing it to make them happy."

"It would also make *me* happy."

That was different, but that wasn't the reason either. "It's just important for me to do." I was glad she didn't ask me to explain it any more because I didn't understand it myself. Why did I want to talk to this guy? I'd interviewed him already. Certainly enough to get the extra marks. Mrs. Watkins hadn't said anything about how long the interview should be and I *had* spoken to him. And especially after the way he walked away last night, how did I know he'd even talk to me? Of course, that was also assuming I could find him to begin with.

"Are you feeling well?" Berta asked.

"Sure, I feel fine. Why?"

"You hardly touched your breakfast."

"I wasn't that hungry." Actually I was too nervous to eat.

"And you were up last night ... a few times."

"How did you know?" I asked, surprised she was aware of it.

"I hear noises ... I wake up."

"I'm sorry," I apologized. "I tried to be quiet ... I'm sorry I woke you up."

"You were quiet," Berta said. "But I hear even quiet noises in the middle of the night."

I knew all about Berta and her nights. She often took a little nap, a siesta, during the afternoon to make up for difficulties getting to sleep. I used to think she stayed up late to watch the Spanish soap operas on cable but it was more than that. She just couldn't sleep. My mother said some people were like that, just natural nighthawks.

"I checked on you when I was up," she said.

"You did?"

"I saw the light on and peeked into your room. Once you were just staring out the window ... another time at the computer."

I hadn't been able to sleep either. I'd gone back to the computer a few times and looked up more information. What I'd found hadn't settled my mind, only disturbed it more.

"More school work," I lied.

Berta half turned so she kept one eye on the road but could cast a half gaze on me. She didn't have to say a word.

"Sort of school work. Things I was learning about bothered me. Have you heard of Rwanda?"

"*Si.* Terrible what happened."

"You know about it?"

"I read. I remember. Some things are hard to forget."

"But I didn't know about it. How could I not know *anything*?" I asked.

"No one knows everything. Things like that they are not taught to children ... best to protect them from these things."

"Protect them? How does not telling somebody protect them?" I asked.

Berta shrugged. "This traffic ... this jammed traffic ... is so bad. Your parents go through it every day ... no wonder they come home with bad moods some days."

"Some days? How about *most* days?" I snapped.

"Some days," Berta said firmly. "Your mama and papa are good people. They have always treated me very well."

I was going to say something but I didn't. I guess they did treat Berta well ... but why shouldn't they? She did everything for us. She held our family together.

"You can let me off anywhere along here," I said. We were right beside the park.

"I've come this far. I'll drive you right to where you need to go."

"This is where I'm going."

She gave me a quick but piercing look. She looked confused and worried. She slowed down and pulled the car over to the side of the road.

"Thanks a lot, Berta," I said. I started to climb out when she reached over and took me by the arm.

"Eon?" she asked.

"It's okay. I'm interviewing a street person. He lives here in the park."

She shook her head. "This is safe, no?"

"There's nothing to worry about. I'll be fine. Honest."

She released her grip and slipped her arm around me, pulling me all the way into the car and giving me a little hug. "I will worry—that is my job. Be careful, *carino mio*."

"I'll be fine." I climbed out and then leaned back into the car. "Thanks."

"It is nothing, just a drive."

"Thanks for that as well." I closed the door and headed into the park. I looked back and watched as she slowly edged back into the flow of traffic. I watched her little car—bright green with even brighter spots of orange rust on the back fender—merge into the flow of the river of cars. The little ceramic dog with the bobbing head in the back window waved to me and I couldn't help smiling back—it always made me smile. The little car disappeared among the larger cars and trucks and she was gone. I always liked being in her car—more than I liked being in any of my parents' fancy cars.

Now that Berta was gone and I'd convinced her that I was going to be fine, I had to work on the other part—convincing *myself* that I'd be okay. I was nervous. More than nervous. Partly I was anxious about talking to him, wondering if he'd even talk to me or how he'd react. Partly I was just concerned about being in this park. It was day but that didn't mean there wouldn't be people here to cause me grief. People like those three punks I'd run into the first time.

I was dressed down, in old shoes and jacket, hoping nobody would bother me, but that might not be enough. I was prepared ... just in case. I had a little bit of insurance. I wasn't going to be the only one without some sort of weapon. I patted my left sleeve with my right hand, feeling the metal bar I'd slipped up my sleeve. Thank goodness Berta hadn't noticed it. It was about twenty inches long. I'd found it in the garage, left over from when construction workers put in a new cement patio out back. It was the closest thing I could find to the bar Sarge had had up his sleeve.

I looked all along as I walked, checking out any danger that might be there. There was a lot of activity. There were men and women, business suits and briefcases, rushing along the path on their way to work. Off to the side of the path, the playground was getting a good workout. It was occupied with small children being pushed on swings or swarming over the climber. Clustered around a little bench were six or seven young women. I couldn't help noticing that the children all looked fair-skinned, a couple of them blond, but these women were brown or black. Nannies. Imported to watch children, just like Berta had been for me. Some people might feel sorry for those kids being raised by strangers instead of their parents. I knew better. I just hoped that at least some of them had somebody like Berta ... if that was possible.

I came to a stop to try to get my bearings. I figured I wouldn't find Sarge on the playground or along the paths. If he was even in the park it would be in the trees at that little campsite. I stepped off the path and followed a little track of worn-down dirt leading into the trees. I checked the bar up my sleeve, pulling it out an inch or two. Somehow it seemed more reassuring to not just feel it but see it. The cold metal against my fingers felt good.

This part of the path looked somewhat familiar. This was the path Mac and I had taken the other night. At least it *looked* like it, but there could be dozens of these throughout the park for all I knew. I ducked to get under some overhanging branches. I looked back. The playground, the main path, and the people walking along it were all out of sight now. Funny, I was in the very middle of a city of over three million people but I was now out of sight of them all. I reached for the metal bar again. Maybe I'd just keep my hand on it.

I kept moving. The path dipped and twisted and I was just starting to think that I'd gone the wrong way when I caught a glimpse of colour through the bushes—red—the colour of the tent canvas. I pushed back the last line of branches and stepped into the clearing. There were six—no seven—tents. It was different to see them in the light of day. It all seemed more real ... as real as a bunch of tents in the middle of a park in the middle of the city could be.

The tents were different sizes, shapes, and colours. A couple looked almost new. One was leaning over at a strange angle and looked like it would tumble over if a little breeze came up. The clearing was a fair size, but all the tents were huddled at one end. They looked like they had been chased to the far end and then clustered together for protection. Maybe they were.

I watched as a thin wisp of smoke gently rose from the still-smouldering firepit into the sky and—There was somebody sitting in one of the chairs around the fire. He struggled to his feet—it was him! He walked—no, stumbled—over to the fire and tossed on a log, releasing a cloud of dust and smoke into the air. As he turned back around, he saw me. He waved and I waved back. Any thought I had of leaving was over. Now that I was here and he'd seen me, what was I going to say? I hadn't thought through this part very well. It would have been easier to just hope he showed up tonight for a meal.

"How are you?" he called out.

"Okay ... I hope I'm not bothering you," I apologized.

"Of course you're not. I was hoping to talk to you."

"You wanted to talk to me?"

He nodded. "I was going to come by for a meal tonight so I could apologize to you."

"But I came to apologize to *you*!"

"To me ... What for?" he asked.

"I didn't know about what happened. I should have known," I explained.

He shook his head. "People don't know, or if they knew they've forgotten. I shouldn't have walked away like that. You did nothing wrong. It just brought back memories ... things I didn't want to think about." He paused. "Do you have more questions you want to ask?"

"A couple more," I answered. "If that would be okay?"

He sat back down. He directed me to a second lawn chair across from him. It sagged under my weight and I thought for a second I was going to tumble over.

"I wouldn't want to cost you any marks," he said. He sounded serious but I could tell from his voice that he was teasing me. "Go ahead so you can finish your assignment."

"This isn't for school any more. After we talked I went home and I read about Rwanda, about what happened, and I just needed to know more ... None of it seemed real."

"I was there and it doesn't seem real to me." He paused. "Do you read the Bible much?" he asked.

His question threw me. "No ... not much." I guess not ever was not much.

"But you know about the Garden of Eden, right?"

"Of course."

"That's what Rwanda was. It was like the Garden of Eden ... at least before the killings."

He said the last words so softly that I could hardly hear him. It was like he had been telling me a secret or it had been a thought that had inadvertently escaped his lips.

We sat there on opposite sides of the little firepit, not speaking. He stared off into the distance and I watched the smoke from the fire curl up and disappear. There wasn't a cloud in the sky. It was a brilliant blue—blue like the Rwandan flag, like the berets of the peacekeepers. There wasn't a sound. Not traffic, not birds, not even wind in the trees. Just silence.

"One day you're there, trying to help, thinking that you *can* help, that you can be part of making a difference for these people, and then the next … you're nothing more than a witness to acts of unspeakable evil." He paused. "And you're helpless to stop it."

His hands were shaking—actually, all of him looked to be shaking. He stared past me off in the distance. He started fumbling around, checking his pockets. He pulled out a package of matches and then continued to search, but came up empty.

"I need a smoke," he said. "You don't have a smoke … That's right, you don't smoke."

"I don't smoke, but I do have some cigarettes."

I reached into my pocket and pulled out a fresh, new, unopened package of cigarettes. I'd had Berta stop at a store on the way so I could get some gum. I'd picked up the cigarettes while she waited in the car. I wanted to give them to him the way Mac gave cigarettes to people. It seemed to work for him.

"Here," I said as I held them out.

"But if you don't smoke, why do you have cigarettes?" he asked.

"I knew you smoked and I thought you could use them," I explained.

"That was nice of you."

"That's no problem. You'll have cigarettes for the whole day."

"Afraid they won't last that long. As soon as the guys get up I'll be sharing with them," he said, gesturing to the tent.

"How many people are here?"

"I think ten. Might be twelve. Could be fourteen. I didn't count. We just make space for whoever needs a place. We share. That's how we get by."

I stood up to give him the package. He reached over and then grabbed me by the arm and held on, catching me completely by surprise. My heart leapt into my throat, and I tried to pull away but he held me firm. He was strong, his grip vice-like.

"What do you have here?" he asked, holding the arm that held the bar up my sleeve.

"N-n-nothing," I stammered. He released his grip and I practically tumbled over backwards before I regained my balance.

"Seems like something," he said.

Slowly, hesitantly, I pulled the bar free, revealing it inch by inch, until I held the whole thing in my hand. What was he going to say to me?

"Give it here," he said, holding out his hand.

Reluctantly I handed it to him. He held it up, slowly turning it around, looking at it from all angles.

"Good weight. Good length." He handed it back to me.

"I thought that I should have something … It's sort of like the one you have," I said, trying to explain and excuse myself.

"They say imitation is a form of flattery. It's been a while since anybody wanted to imitate me."

"I just thought it would be smart for me to have something. I can't just hope that you'll be there again if I need you."

"Smart to be prepared. Not so smart if the police see it. You'd be charged with a weapons offence. Besides, it's only helpful if you're planning on using it—were you?"

"I was hoping I wouldn't have to."

"But if you did have to?" he persisted.

I shook my head. "I'm not sure. If I had to … maybe … probably … I hope."

"That's probably the best answer. You just don't know. You can never predict your reactions until you're in a situation, especially one involving life and death … especially if that death involved *your* life."

I knew he'd been in those situations. I'd only read about them or seen them on TV or the movies.

Sarge picked up the cigarette package, which had fallen in his lap. With shaking hands he peeled off the cellophane wrapping, removed a cigarette, and put it in his mouth. He struck a match and tried to connect the shaking end with the cigarette. They met and the end of the cigarette started to glow, and he exhaled a puff of smoke.

"That's good," he said as he inhaled another drag of the cigarette. "Now all I need is something to eat. Have you had breakfast?" he asked.

"No."

"Hungry?"

"I am now."

"Come on," he said as he got up. "I know where we can get a bite. You like bagels?"

"Sure … who doesn't?"

"This place has the best bagels. You ever had a Montreal bagel?" he asked.

"I've been to Montreal. I just don't know if I ate a bagel when I was there."

He laughed. "It isn't the location. It's the way they're made. Sweeter, different dough. You're going to like it."

He got up from his seat. "Come, let's go and eat."

I got up from my chair. I slipped the metal bar back up my sleeve and quickly caught up to him as he retraced the steps I'd taken earlier that morning. I pressed a hand into my pocket to make sure I still had money. I felt the bills—three five-dollar bills. I didn't have my wallet with me. I'd deliberately left that safely on the top of my dresser. I'd offer to pay for our breakfast. I was going to tell him that when I realized that I didn't even know his real name.

"I was wondering, should I call you Sarge?" I asked.

He smiled. "You could, but the boys they call me Jack."

"Okay, sure … Jack. I was wondering, how long have you lived in the park?"

"Most of the winter."

"And nobody bothers you?"

"Who would bother us?" he asked.

"I don't know, the parks people or maybe the police."

"They know we're there, but they just leave us alone."

"And they don't try to make you move?"

"We only burn deadfall, make sure the fire is tended, and as long as we stay out of sight they leave us alone. That's important, staying out of sight. The people driving by, walking in the park, up in those big buildings doing important business, as long as they don't see us they can pretend we don't exist."

That was exactly what Mac had said to me. As long as you didn't see something you didn't have to deal with it.

"By the way, what day is it today?"

"Thursday."

"Sometimes I lose track of the days, but I thought it looked too busy, too much traffic, to be a weekend," he said. Then he turned to me and slowed down a bit. "If it's Thursday what are you doing here instead of at school?"

"I guess I should be in school," I said reluctantly.

"Be careful," he said as he started to cross the street. We dodged cars as we crossed. He cut across the parking lot of a donut shop. There was a long line of cars waiting at the drive-through window.

"Here it is. Best bagels around," Jack said.

I could see through the front window that a lot of people agreed with him because there was an equally long line at the counter inside. I grabbed the front door, holding it open for Jack and—

"Not that way. Come," he said, motioning for me to follow.

We circled around the side. Was there another entrance? The back of the building certainly wasn't as fancy as the front. There were boarded-up windows and a big brown door with a mass of graffiti marking the territory, some garbage cans and a big green dumpster.

"Let's see what they're serving for breakfast," Jack said. He took the lid of the dumpster and swung it up.

I stopped dead in my tracks, stunned.

"Hold this for me."

"What?" I asked in shock.

"Hold the lid, so I can look inside."

"You're not serious, are you? You're not going to eat from the dumpster."

"Why not?"

"I have money," I said, digging into my pocket. "I was going to buy us breakfast ... inside ... we don't have to eat from the garbage."

"I can't take your money. Besides, it's not just me. I'm hoping I can bring back something for everybody. Take the lid so I can search."

I stumbled forward, putting the money back in my pocket and grabbing the big plastic lid, holding it up. Jack shuffled around cardboard boxes, and papers and—

"Here it is!" he said, holding up a large, clear plastic bag. It was filled with donuts and muffins and bagels. There had to be three or four dozen. As he started to look in the bag I lowered the lid. I looked around, trying to see if anybody had noticed what we'd done.

"What do you want?" he asked as he sat down on the curb and started to undo the bag.

"Should you be doing that here?" I asked. "What if somebody came out of the donut store?"

"Then I'd say thank you."

"But wouldn't they get mad at you?"

He shook his head. "They know what I'm doing. How did you think I knew to look? A couple of the people who work here, they told me to look, told me there'd be something there most days."

"Why would they do that?" I asked.

"It isn't like they can sell them. These are two days old. The fresh ones they sell. The day-olds they put in a bag and sell at half price. These are the ones they couldn't sell at half price so they toss them. So what do you want?"

"I don't know … Maybe I shouldn't have anything … just to make sure there's enough for everybody else," I said, trying to provide a legitimate excuse to avoid eating from a dumpster without offending him.

"You suit yourself, but you don't have to worry, they're fine. They might have been in a dumpster but they were inside a sealed plastic bag. Besides, a couple of days old isn't bad. Your parents buy a bag of bagels at the grocery store. It hangs around for three, four, maybe five days before the last one is eaten. Try one," he said, holding the bag out.

I didn't have much choice. If I turned it down I'd run the risk of offending him. Gingerly, reluctantly, hesitantly, I reached into the bag and removed a bagel. There were little bits of what I hoped were blueberries poking through the surface. I pressed a finger against it. It didn't feel stale. I took a small bite. It tasted okay. It tasted good. Sweet.

"Montreal bagel. Reminds me of home."

"You're from Montreal?" I asked.

"I've lived everywhere, but my family is originally from Montreal if you go back far enough. Come, let's get back." He started walking. "You asked why those people put these out for us," Jack said. "You want to know the reason?"

I nodded my head.

"I read a lot. Magazines, newspapers, books. You'd be amazed how many things are thrown out."

I pictured him dumpster-diving for books as well as bagels.

"So I'm reading this science magazine about these researchers who were mapping the genetic codes of different animals, including man. And they found that there wasn't that much difference between animals that they'd always thought were completely different. Bees and birds, horses and hyenas, humans and chimpanzees."

What did any of this have to do with why people gave him two-day-old donuts and bagels?

"Humans and chimpanzees share over ninety-eight percent of the same genetic material. The things that make one a chimp and the other a man constitute less than two percent. Isn't that amazing?"

"Yeah, I guess," I said, still not understanding what point he was trying to make.

"So if you and a monkey share so much, just imagine how much you and I must share, or how much we both share with a man in China. We're all basically the same. Think how little difference there is between any of us."

"That makes sense. The difference must be small. Way, way less than one percent, way less."

"Way less. So me and those people who work in the donut store, we're basically the same. Them doing something nice for me is just like them helping a member of their family. We're all in this together. We're all part of the same family. And that's what makes Rwanda so hard for me to believe."

"What do you mean?"

"The people in Rwanda, the three tribal groups—"

"Three? I thought there were just two ... the Tutsi and the Hu ... the Hu—"

"The Hutus," he said. "You did look things up, didn't you?"

I nodded my head.

"The Hutus make up the majority of the people, close to eighty percent. The Tutsi make up around fifteen percent and then there's a third group, the Twa."

"I didn't know about them."

"Small, only a percent. And all around, in neighbouring countries, are Tutsi who were displaced, living in other countries—Tanzania, Burundi, Uganda, Zaire, the Congo. But these groups of people, living side by side together in the Garden of Eden since the dawn of time, how different could any of them be from each other? How much difference could there be between a Hutu and a Tutsi?"

"Nothing, I guess," I said.

"But that nothing was enough." He shook his head. "Have you ever seen a dead person?"

"On TV, on the news." I'd never even been to a funeral.

"I'd seen bodies before. I've lived a long time. I've served in the military in places around the world, places where death isn't sanitized and hidden away like it is in this country. Death is a part of life."

We crossed the street. The traffic was a little lighter as morning rush hour was starting to wind down.

"But seeing death before didn't prepare me for what I saw there. Nothing *could* prepare me—or anybody else. I'd never seen so much death, death happening in so many ways."

"Like with a machete?" I asked, thinking back to what he'd said to me the first time we had met.

He nodded. "Yes, with a machete, and knives, guns and rockets and grenades. Do you believe in Heaven?" he asked suddenly.

"Heaven ... do you mean like clouds and pearly gates and harps?"

"I'm not sure what it will look like but I know it exists," he said. "Do you know why I'm so sure?"

I shook my head.

"I know there must be a Heaven because I've seen Hell. Sometimes it was so hot it almost burned my lungs when I inhaled. Other times it was so cold that my blood nearly froze. I've seen Hell. I've *been* in Hell ... here and in Rwanda. And because of that, because I *know* there is a Hell, I'm positive there must be a Heaven."

All the time he'd been talking he'd been looking straight ahead, no hint of expression on his face.

He stopped in the middle of the small wooden bridge spanning a creek that cut through the park. "Do you know what I think of every time I cross over this bridge?"

Of course I didn't know, but I didn't think he expected an answer.

"I think of bodies. A river full of bloated human bodies, dumped in a river, so thick that they formed a blockage across the river where it went under a bridge. And people had to haul those bodies out, drag them up onto the shore and dump them back into the river on the other side of the bridge to stop that log-jam of human beings from causing a flood. And each time they pulled out a body, another drifted down the river to take its place."

I stared down at the creek. There was a grocery cart embedded in the mud of the bank, and a white plastic bag, caught in the current, twisted and turned as it floated along with the current and then disappeared under our feet. But as Jack stood there, staring down, I knew he hadn't seen the plastic bag. He was seeing those bodies floating by ... He was seeing Hell.

Twelve

I'D TAKEN A BUS, a commuter train, and then finally a taxi to get back to school by noon. I wanted to get there in time for civics—the class before lunch. I signed in at the office—told them I'd had an appointment, and then headed off for class. I got there late but still got there. I quietly slipped in the door. Mrs. Watkins was writing on the board. She looked over and gave me a disdainful glare. She continued writing and talking. The only open seats were—of course—in the front row. Was this going to be my new seat?

"Nice of you to join us, Mr. Blackburn," Mrs. Watkins said as she turned away from the board.

"Sorry I'm late. I was finishing up my interview ... the one you wanted me to do."

"With the soldier?"

"Retired soldier ... special operations."

"Excellent! So please, tell us what he said, give us an oral report."

I was taken aback. I hadn't seen that coming. I thought I could write something up and hand it in. Slowly I got to my feet as Mrs. Watkins took a seat at her desk in the corner. What was I going to say, where was I going to start?

"I interviewed a gentleman who was a sergeant in the armed forces. His name is Jack. He said he was stationed at bases around the country but that he was also part of missions around the world." I reached down and grabbed my notebook. I'd used the train ride to finish transcribing my notes into it. "He was in the military for twenty-four years. It was sort of like the family business. His father was in the military and his grandfather. Jack said that he felt like he was doing the right thing, defending our country and trying to help people. He was part of United Nations peacekeeping missions in different countries, countries like Haiti and Bosnia and the Middle East and Rwanda."

"Rwanda?" Mrs. Watkins said. "I didn't know there were any Canadians in Rwanda."

"There were eventually over forty countries that sent soldiers. There weren't many Canadians, but some. The commander was a Canadian during the genocide."

"The genocide," Mrs. Watkins said softly as she stood up. "Does anybody know what a genocide is?"

"Isn't that when a lot of people get killed?" a girl answered.

"In most armed conflicts people get killed. We consider it an acceptable part of war when those who are killed are the combatants, the soldiers. We consider it far less acceptable when innocents, civilians, are killed. The term used today is collateral casualties. That basically means that they were killed because they were in the wrong place and were killed as one set of soldiers attempted to kill soldiers on the opposing side. With a genocide, the death of civilians is not accidental. The civilians *are* the targets. Genocide is a methodical, deliberate attempt to kill civilians, especially those who are of a particular or specific ethnic, religious, or racial group."

"Like the Holocaust," somebody said.

We'd studied the Holocaust in grade eight and I didn't think there was anybody who didn't know at least something about that. I'd even read a couple of books—sort of historical fiction about kids who were in the Holocaust.

"The Holocaust was one act of genocide," Mrs. Watkins agreed. "In World War II the Nazi party under the direction of its leader, Adolf Hitler, decided to kill all persons who were Jewish. Men, women, small children, old people, babes in arms, were subject to a systematic attempt to annihilate an entire group of people. While there are some debates concerning the exact number, it is without question a fact that at least six million Jews were killed. They were shot, electrocuted, killed with explosives, and in the best-known example, slaughtered by the use of gas in the concentration camps."

"It's so hard to believe," another girl said. "What made them do that … act like that? What made them so full of hate?"

"If it was just the Nazis it would be one thing," Mrs. Watkins said. "The Holocaust is the largest and best-known genocide of the twentieth century but it was not the only, or the first, or the last." Mrs. Watkins took a sip from her cup. "In a period between 1915 and 1923 there were over 1.5 million Armenians killed. The entire land mass of Asia Minor was expunged of all Armenians. They were either killed or forced to leave, and many of those forced to leave died of disease and starvation."

"Who killed them?" somebody asked.

"Turks. It was a genocide against Armenian Christians by Turkish Muslims."

"But how could that take place? Didn't somebody try to stop them?" Jeremy asked.

"At first nobody even noticed. It wasn't like today with mass communications and satellites and Internet and CNN," Mrs. Watkins explained. "And when it was discovered there were so many other things going on with World War I and then there was confusion about who in fact should, or could, intervene."

"That was a long time ago," somebody else observed.

"It was. How about the killing fields of Cambodia?" Mrs. Watkins asked.

"Wasn't that a movie?" Kelsey asked.

"It was. A movie about the genocide in Cambodia in the seventies when the Khmer Rouge movement under the command of Pol Pot killed 1.7 million people. That was over twenty percent of the total population of the country."

"Even that was a long time ago," the same girl said.

"It makes me feel old to realize how long ago you think that is," Mrs. Watson said with a half-smile. "Then there was Yugoslavia. The mass graves are still being discovered today. The final account, the number of different people of different groups who were killed in that genocide, is still unknown ... probably never will be known. And then, most recently, there was the genocide in Rwanda. Ian, do you know anything about what happened?"

"I know the numbers," I said. "Eight hundred thousand people were slaughtered."

One girl gasped. Nobody else even blinked. It was like they didn't hear me or didn't believe me ... or didn't care.

"And do you know when that took place?" Mrs. Watkins asked.

"It happened during a one-hundred-day period in 1994."

"That can't be right," a boy at the back said. "We would have heard about it."

"It did happen," Mrs. Watkins said. "This soldier—Jack—you said he was there."

I nodded my head. "He was there, but he told me it was hard even for him to believe it. He told me about people being attacked with machetes ... about rivers being clogged with bodies ... other horrible things."

I could tell by the expressions of a couple of the girls in the front that they were upset or disgusted.

"Do we *have* to talk about this?" a girl asked.

"We don't have to talk about anything," Mrs. Watkins said. "But please explain to me why we shouldn't talk about this?"

"Well ... it's just so ... so ... gross."

"And upsetting," another girl added.

"Maybe that's why we should talk about it," Mrs. Watkins said. "I remember hearing a minister say that the best thing a sermon could ever do was comfort the troubled and trouble the comfortable. I think it's important to know about the world around us ... the larger world beyond MTV and the mall." She took another sip from her mug and then turned directly to me. "Ian, is this soldier a friend of the family?"

"No. I just know him."

"How do you know him?" Mrs. Watkins persisted.

I really didn't want to answer, but I didn't have much choice. "I know him from the soup kitchen."

"Does he do volunteer work there too?" she asked.

"No ... he ... he eats there."

"He's a street person?" Mrs. Watkins asked.

"Yeah."

"He's a *bum*?" Jason squealed and then started to laugh. "You got all your information from a bum!"

"He lives on the street, but he's not a bum!" I snapped. "And you better shut your face right now or I'm going to—"

Mrs. Watkins was instantly at my side as I started to get out of my seat. She stepped in front of me, heading me off.

"Nobody is calling anybody anything. I want an apology. Now!"

"I'm sorry ... I didn't mean nothin'," Jason mumbled.

Good. Nobody was going to call Jack a bum or—

"Now your turn, Ian," Mrs. Watkins said.

"My turn to what?" I asked.

"To apologize. Nobody is either calling somebody names *or* threatening to harm them. That's how wars, and genocide, begin."

I mumbled an apology.

"But how does somebody go from being in the armed forces to being a street person?" a girl asked.

"That's not as far a fall as you might think. People in all walks of life can end up on the streets," Mrs. Watkins said. "Alcoholism and mental illness don't discriminate between people. The biggest difference between those who overcome and those who succumb isn't the person who is afflicted but the people who surround that individual ... the supports that allow them to heal and regain their equilibrium. Some people are just lucky enough to have somebody there to help them. You know, sometimes it only takes one person." She took another sip from her coffee. "Does anybody know what groups Hitler targeted before the Jews?"

There was no answer.

"The mentally ill and the homeless," she said. "They were the first people he sterilized, rounded up, and exterminated. He was allowed to get away with that so he moved on to the next group. Who knows how history would have been changed if there had been a national or international reaction, outrage? Maybe he never would have cemented his power, maybe World War II never would have happened. But who was going to object to his actions? It was just a bunch of crazy, homeless people. Maybe not worthless, but certainly worth less," she said, echoing the phrase from the last class.

Mrs. Watkins took another sip from her bottomless cup. I wanted to say something, but I just didn't know what to say. No one else seemed to know what to say either. The whole room was deadly silent. There wasn't even the sound of shifting feet or shuffling papers. Nothing.

"Did anybody here drop off flowers in memory of Crystal?" Mrs. Watkins asked.

A half-dozen girls put up their hands. Crystal was a nine-year-old girl who had been abducted, sexually assaulted, killed, and her body dumped in a park by the lake. It had happened half a year before. It was awful ... just awful. I could so clearly picture her—at least the photographs of her that had been in the papers and on the newscasts. At the spot where her body had been found people had started to drop off flowers and stuffed animals. These people—most had to be strangers—came, cried, and then left. I'd seen it on the news. It had become a virtual garden of flowers, a mountain of stuffed animals.

"Did any of you girls know Crystal?" Mrs. Watkins asked.

They all shook their heads.

"Why did you bring flowers?" she asked.

"I brought a teddy bear," one of the girls said.

"Fine. Why did you bring *anything*?" Mrs. Watkins asked.

"I just wanted to say how sorry I was," the teddy bear girl replied.

"Yeah, so the family would know that people cared," added another.

"How about you, Cindy?" Mrs. Watson asked.

"I ... I don't really know why I did it. I just wanted to try to ... I don't know ... This is going to sound stupid."

"It won't, I'm sure. Just say it," Mrs. Watkins said.

"I just wanted to do something kind to try to make it better," she said.

"A small act of kindness, of goodness, to try to counter the evil that was done," Mrs. Watkins said.

"But it wasn't like I could fix it or make it better," Cindy said.

"You're partially right. You couldn't fix it, but you did make it a little bit better. A random act of kindness often sends ripples that have a positive effect," Mrs. Watkins said.

"I saw her mother being interviewed. She said she was thankful to all those people who had dropped by," another girl said.

"I was wondering, did anybody think about giving flowers for the eight hundred thousand people who were killed in Rwanda?" Mrs. Watkins asked.

"We didn't even *know* about Rwanda," Cindy said.

"You do now. You already knew about the Holocaust and the millions killed. And I've now told you about the 1.5 million people killed in the Armenian genocide and the 1.7 million people who were victims of the Cambodia killing fields, and the tens of thousands killed in the ethnic cleansing in Yugoslavia. But you can't grieve for these countless victims because they are just a number, a number so large it can't be comprehended." She swirled the coffee in her mug but didn't sip from it. "One death is a tragedy; a million is a statistic. Does anybody know what that means?" she asked.

"I do," I said. "The death of Crystal is a tragedy because we know her—at least we *feel* like we know her, because we can picture her, we know about her family, we've seen her mother on the news crying. But the million people, we don't know them so we don't care about what happened to them. A million is just a number, a statistic."

"Perfectly said, Ian. But each of those million was a living, breathing, feeling human being, each as much a person as Crystal. And as long as they remain unknown, separated from us by time or distance or situation, we don't have to know them. They *remain* a statistic."

The entire room was so silent that I could hear the ticking of the clock hanging on the back wall.

"Does anybody know who said that?" Mrs. Watkins asked.

"You, right now," Jeremy joked.

Mrs. Watkins let out a deep, long sigh. "Does anybody know who *originally* said it?"

It had to be like Plato or Socrates or some old-time Greek philosopher, or maybe Shakespeare, he was always saying things like that, or maybe Mark Twain or—

"Joseph Stalin," Mrs. Watkins said.

"Who's that?"

"He was the leader of the Communist Party in Russia. Under his orders millions upon millions of his fellow Russians were executed." She paused. "Millions and millions. He knew enough to make sure they were only statistics."

Thirteen

FINDING MORE INFORMATION about the genocide had been easy. Actually, it was amazing just how much information was readily available. So much information and none of us had known anything about it.

What I was finding hard was locating information that didn't just involve numbers, facts, and figures. Eight hundred thousand people had been slaughtered. I knew the number—the statistic—but I didn't know about one individual person who made up those numbers. It was just one large, faceless, anonymous black mass. How could the human mind hope to comprehend what a number that big even meant? I needed to see a picture, look into somebody's eyes the way I had looked into Crystal's eyes in those pictures in the paper. The way I could *still* look into her eyes whenever I closed my eyes or called on her memory. I needed to do this, to know something about somebody who had been killed in Rwanda. I didn't exactly understand why I needed to do this, but I did. Somehow I needed to not let them just be statistics, so here I was, back at my computer.

I clicked from page to page, site to site. More of the same. Maps, facts, figures, numbers, political discussion, but no— I stopped. Staring back at me were the soft brown eyes of a boy. He could have been ten or twelve or fourteen. I couldn't tell. He had a gentle smile and was dressed in a starched white shirt and tie and there was something wrong with his arm … the sleeve was wrong. Was it just the angle of the picture or was he hiding his arm behind him or … it was gone. It just wasn't there … his left arm was missing. Under his picture was a title: Witness to a Genocide.

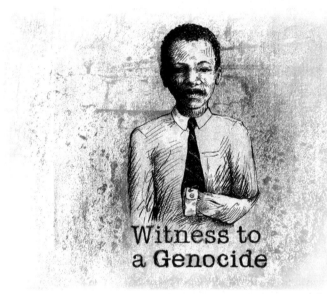

I hesitated for a second, then another. Was this what I was looking for? Now that I'd maybe found it, I wasn't sure I wanted to. I looked deep into his eyes. I knew I owed it to him—I owed it to myself to go further. I scrolled down the page. As the text was revealed at the bottom, his face disappeared from the top of the screen.

My name is Jacob. I lived in Kigali with my family. My mother and my father and my three brothers and two sisters. And in the next house lived my mother's parents and her sisters lived beside that, with all my cousins. It was April the 9th. I know the day because it was my birthday the next day. I was going to turn eleven. I was excited. I went to bed waiting for my birthday to come. I was so excited that I had trouble sleeping. My parents had trouble sleeping too but for a different reason. They were scared. I knew that. Scared of what we had heard. That people were hurting other people. Hutus harming Tutsi. My family is Tutsi. I was a little scared too, but not too much. My father and my uncles and my big cousins and my oldest brother were all around. Nobody could hurt me with them to protect me. In the night, I don't know what time, I heard the sounds on the street. Screaming and yelling but also it sounded like laughter and music—loud music. It sounded like a party, like somebody was celebrating. And then I heard louder screaming, sounding like it was coming from right inside my house, and before I could even think the door of my room was thrown open and dark figures rushed into the room. I was grabbed by the arm and by the hair and dragged off my sleeping mat and pulled into the main room. The room was filled with people, dozens and dozens of strangers. They were yelling and screaming. Some had spears, others pieces of wood or pipe, and some had machetes. My mother was there, and my father and all my brothers and sisters. They were being held and struck! I couldn't believe it, it was like a nightmare. We were all dragged into the street. I was punched and kicked as I was dragged along, my arm twisting and turning, my head aching, my stomach screaming out so much I thought I was going to be sick. Outside, the street was filled with even more people—more people than I had ever seen. And among these strangers I saw other members of my family, my grand-mother, my cousins, my uncles and aunts, all being held, and kicked, and hit with sticks. And then I saw my grandfather, lying on the ground, not moving, his clothes painted with blood. Then I felt something, like a burning, searing pain in my arm and I looked down and my arm—the whole arm from above the elbow was gone! There was a man, holding a machete in one hand and the jagged remains of my arm in the other! I staggered backward and fell over, clasping the stump of my arm with my other hand, the blood flowing, streaming. I tried to cry out for my mother or father when the air became filled with screams. And from the ground where I lay I saw the man, still holding my arm, waving it in the faces of my parents. My father struggled to get free and my mother cried out but they started to hit them ... more and more blows with fists and kicks and sticks and then my mother was struck with a machete and fell to the ground, blood gushing from the slash across her face. I tried to get up but I was kicked and then somebody stomped on me and then something heavy, a body, tumbled on top of me. I started to struggle to move but I didn't have the strength and somehow it felt safe to be underneath, protected. I heard screams. I knew the voices. Voices of my cousins and my sisters and my brothers crying out in pain. And along with those voices there were other people, cheering, laughing, and the sound of music kept on playing. I couldn't see, pinned beneath the body, and I closed my eyes. I knew that if I screamed or cried out for help that nobody could come to save me—it would just draw attention. My only hope to not die was to have them think that I already was dead. I felt weaker and weaker and then nothing.

When I woke up I was lying on a mat. There was bright light. I looked around. I didn't know where I was but I saw other people lying around on mats all around me. I tried to get up, push myself up, and then I saw my arm—what was left of my arm—and I slumped to the ground. That was when the nurse came. She told me I was in a hospital. I asked her about my family. She didn't want to say, but I kept asking and asking. Even before she answered, I knew. Finally she told me.

I was found on the street, trapped beneath a body. Everybody else—all of my family, all of my neighbours—were dead. The street was silent. They thought I was dead too. But I wasn't. And I'm not. And I'm alive to tell my story. This is what happened to me. This is true. This is my story.

I tried to scroll back up the page. My hand was shaking. I moved up until Jacob's picture was once again on the screen. I looked at him. I saw the sleeve neatly pinned to his starched white shirt. And then I looked deep into his eyes. Jacob wasn't a statistic. He was a person.

I'D TRIED to get to sleep for a long time. Each time I closed my eyes I saw Jacob's. I had wanted to know about a person. Now I knew and I wished I didn't. I couldn't get his picture out of my mind. I couldn't get the story out of my mind. I looked at the dim outline of my door and thought about Jacob lying in his bed, and those men—those evil devils—bursting in through the door.

My mouth was dry. I sat up, reached over, and took a sip from the glass of Coke that sat on my night table. Warm, flat, caffeine-filled liquid. That would really help me get to sleep. All it did was confirm that I needed to go to the bathroom.

I climbed out of bed and went to the bathroom. I flipped up the seat and it clanked noisily against the back of the tank. As I stood there relieving myself I heard a sound—music and voices from outside on the street. I stopped and looked out the window. It was a car, radio blaring, racing away. I watched as the tail lights disappeared around the corner.

Suddenly my whole body felt uneasy, anxious, like I was on pins and needles. I felt my breath catch in my throat. Something was wrong, I didn't know what, but something ... then I realized. The voices, the music outside my bedroom ... that was what Jacob had heard outside his room before he was grabbed and dragged outside ... before his arm was cut off ... before all of his family was killed.

I took a deep breath. Okay, this wasn't good, but at least I knew why I was feeling so anxious. But even though I knew, my heart wasn't slowing down, and I wasn't feeling any better. Maybe a glass of milk would help.

I walked out of the bathroom, through my bedroom, opened the door and peered into the hall. It was silent and dark. The only light was a dim glow leaking up the stairs from the night light in the little bathroom down by the kitchen. Slowly, on bare feet, I moved along the hallway. My parents' bedroom door was slightly ajar. I started to pass by, when I stopped. I listened at the door. Silence. Slowly I pushed open the door. It was dark, but I looked hard until I could make out two lumps under the covers. They were in bed ... But of course they were in bed—where else would they be?

I padded down the stairs, guided and safeguarded by the little night light. I flicked on the light in the kitchen and then instantly turned it back off again. The curtains were open and somehow I'd felt open, exposed to anybody outside who was watching or ... This was stupid. Nobody was outside, nobody was watching. I turned the light back on, opened the fridge, and grabbed the carton of milk. I took a big chug from the carton. My mother hated when I did that. She was asleep, so what was she going to say or know or do? I took another gulp.

I walked over to the back door. I jiggled the door handle just to make sure it was locked. Of course it was locked. Berta always made sure the place was sealed up as tight as a drum every night. She was almost paranoid about things like that so there was no need to check … just like there was no need to check the front door or the door that led out of the garage and into the house. I took another drink from the carton, tipping it back and draining the last bit of milk. I put the empty carton down on the kitchen counter. Then I went to check the front and garage doors.

Fourteen

THE SUN BEAT DOWN strongly and brightly. It felt more like midday in the summer than four in the afternoon in April. But that was how this country went—directly from way too cold to far too hot. Spring lasted about two days.

I was feeling so hot that I wanted to take off my jacket but figured it was best to leave it on. Better to fit in. All the street people still had on their coats, and toques, and in a couple of cases, gloves. Either they hadn't noticed the change in weather or they were just so grateful not to be cold any more that they wanted to get as hot as possible —maybe store a little heat for when they needed it again next winter.

I'd started to recognize some of the faces under those hats. I'd said hello or nodded to a number of people I'd passed. I'm sure there were more that I knew but it was hard because they never looked up, never made eye contact with the people passing by. Even when they were begging change, their eyes were always focused firmly on the ground.

"Beautiful day, eh?"

I turned toward the voice. It was Jack!

"It's a great day."

"Sun feels good against my face," he said. That was about the only part of him showing. Like everybody else he still wore his thick coat and toque. "You on your way to the Club?"

"Yep."

"Mind if I walk along with you in that direction?"

"Of course not!"

He fell into step beside me.

"So how did things work out with that school assignment ... you know ... the interview?"

"Really well. I'm pretty well guaranteed to pass now."

"And you weren't before?" he asked, sounding concerned.

"It was sort of touch and go for a while," I admitted.

"That doesn't make sense. Smart kid like you should be doing more than just passing, you should be getting good marks."

"That's what my parents keep saying."

"Then it's probably true. So what stops you from getting better marks?" he asked.

"I guess I just don't work hard enough."

"You can't get anywhere without working hard."

It was strange to be given advice about working hard from a man who was living in a tent, but somehow the words rang true coming out of his mouth. I knew that he had been somebody who had worked hard, who had taken pride in what he did. That just made where he was now so much sadder.

"Are you going to eat at the Club tonight?" I asked.

"Maybe."

"But maybe not?"

"We'll see."

"I just figured you were headed in that direction so you were ..." I stopped mid-sentence. "Were you going in this direction or were you thinking it would be safer if I had an escort?"

"Two people are always safer than one," he said with a grin. "Maybe I thought it would make it safer for *me* to be with you."

"Yeah, right, like you need my help."

"We all need help." He was serious now. "Some people just don't get the help they need."

Those last words struck hard. Was he talking about himself and the rest of the people living on the streets, or the people of Rwanda ... those that he couldn't help ... or stranger still, was he talking about me?

"When the sun beats down so brightly I can't help thinking of other places," he said.

"Like Rwanda?" I asked.

"Like Rwanda."

"I just can't believe that I didn't know, that most people *still* don't know what happened there."

He shrugged. "Human nature is to look away from what's unpleasant. Ignorance is bliss. If you look you might have to do something about it."

"I guess. I'm still just trying to understand how all of that could have happened."

"I've spent a lot of years trying to understand it," he said.

"And?"

"If you figure it out you tell me, okay?" he asked.

"I will. I was reading about the convoys," I said.

"You know about the convoys?" he asked, sounding surprised.

"I know a little."

"I'm just surprised you know anything about them."

"I'm interested," I explained.

He stared straight ahead.

I suddenly started to think better of this. Maybe it wasn't fair for me to be bringing it up. "You don't have to talk about it if you don't want. I don't want to bring back any more bad memories."

"You can't bring back what never leaves. But don't worry ... the convoys are one of the few parts I feel good about."

"I'd like to know more about them."

He nodded in agreement but didn't answer right away. I knew he was thinking through his answer—deciding what to say ... and probably just as important, what *not* to say.

"There were certain places, we called them enclaves, where Tutsis were gathered and we could provide them with some level of safety ... some. But we knew that the sharks circling around would eventually stop respecting those very fragile boundaries. It was just a matter of time. We had to move them to the territory controlled by the rebels."

"So you put them in trucks and convoyed them out."

"We did the best we could. You have to understand that our mission in Rwanda—almost all UN missions—are underfunded, undermanned, and under-equipped. Not enough troops or trucks, tents or toilet paper. Not even enough ammunition."

"Ammunition ... you mean like bullets?"

"Like bullets," he said, nodding in agreement. "We didn't have enough rounds of ammunition to survive a battle. We didn't have the men or muscle to force our way out of these enclaves so we had to wait for the right time and hope we could bluff our way through the roadblocks, through the militia and through the mobs."

"That would have been terrifying. I mean, *I* would have been terrified."

"So was I ... so were all of us."

That surprised me—I just didn't think of him as somebody who would be scared.

He glanced at me. "You didn't think I was scared?" he asked.

My expression must have given me away. "I guess not."

"To not be scared would have been to not understand. I was scared when I had to fight those three thugs. Fear is always with you. You just can't let it overwhelm you. I think you would have responded well if you were with me."

"Me? I couldn't even handle those punks in the park."

"Don't underestimate yourself, Ian. I know people. I know you would have acted in an honourable manner."

"The way you acted?" I questioned.

"The way I tried my best to act."

We walked along in silence for a while. I think I'd pushed him too far—or maybe he'd pushed both of us too far.

"How many people do you think were saved by the convoys?"

"Thousands, perhaps tens of thousands of lives."

"You have to feel really good about that."

"It's hard to feel good about saving thousands when hundreds of thousands perished. What we did was just a drop in the bucket."

We continued to walk, but not talk. I knew we were sharing the same thoughts.

"Here you are," Jack said as we stopped in front of the Club. There were already five men waiting by the front doors.

"You want to come in and get something to eat?" I asked. "You could come in with me right now."

"That wouldn't be fair to the guys waiting outside," he said, gesturing to the line.

"It would be different if you came in and offered to help with set-up," I said.

He gave me a questioning look.

"Mac always needs help," I explained.

"You know, I might want to do that some time... but not tonight."

"Some other time. I know Mac would appreciate the help. Maybe you could come back later, talk to him about it and get supper."

He shook his head. "Not tonight. Not hungry."

"Okay. I'll see you later."

"You too. Be safe," he said. Jack started to walk away and then stopped and turned around. "You know, in the beginning my greatest fear was that I would be killed. At the end my greatest fear was that I wouldn't be."

He turned and walked away. I stood there, too stunned to move, too stunned to speak. As he walked away he pulled a bottle out of the inside of his coat and tipped it back to his mouth. Maybe there were things he couldn't forget, but that wasn't stopping him from trying. Either that or trying to die.

Fifteen

I OPENED UP the front door and let in the waiting men. Many of them greeted me with smiles and handshakes. I knew a lot of them. Maybe not by name but I knew them. In the past couple of weeks they'd stopped being a faceless, nameless mass and had started to become individuals. In little bits of conversation with them and things that Mac had told me, I'd gotten to know their stories. Everybody had a story about the path that led them down and onto the streets. And on the way down they were stripped of everything that had once been dear to them: parents, spouses, children, jobs, houses, possessions. Despite it all, somehow against all the odds, some of them had managed to hold on to their dignity. Nobody had come up with that word when Mrs. Watkins had asked for words to describe the homeless, but I saw it all the time.

I let my eyes go to the end of the line, looking for Jack. I hadn't seen him for a week—not since our last conversation—and I was starting to get worried because Mac said he hadn't seen him either.

Mac stood at the counter, serving the chow. Beside him were two older people, two women. They both were well dressed, smiling, and had fancy hair—church ladies.

"He wasn't in the line?" Mac asked as he came out from behind the counter and met me partway across the dining hall.

"No."

"He might still show up tonight."

"Maybe," I agreed.

"Either way, just remember that every day is a blessing."

"A blessing? Are all these church ladies starting to get to you?" I asked.

"I could do worse."

"I guess you could. I just wish Jack would show up."

"You looking for Jack?" asked a man sitting at one of the tables.

"Yeah," I said, turning to face him.

"I doubt he'll be coming here tonight."

"Why not?"

"He's sort of under the weather."

"He's not feeling good?" I asked.

"Actually, he's not feeling much of anything," another man said. "Started drinking a little early today."

"This whole week," the first man added.

The whole week ... Did that have to do with our conversation? Was I just bringing up such bad memories that he had to work harder—*drink* harder—to try to forget?

"Do you know where he is now?" I asked.

"By the tents when I last saw him ... but that was a couple of hours ago. Could still be there. Could be anywhere."

"Not likely," the second said. "He wouldn't be wandering far. If he isn't by the tents, he'll be somewhere in the park."

"Thanks for the information." I turned to Mac. "Can we talk for a minute?"

"Don't see why not. Come on." He walked into the kitchen and I followed.

"Okay, shoot," Mac said.

"I was just wondering ... you've been here a long time. Do you see the same people all the time, you know, year after year?"

"Some of these guys have been coming around as long as I've been here. Some just disappear after a few days or a few weeks."

"What happens to them, the people you don't see any more?" I asked.

"Sometimes they move away to another part of the city or even another city," he said. "Lots of street people like to head out to the West Coast. Weather's milder. You can live outside practically all the time out there."

"So they just move away," I said.

"Some move and some just die. Mortality rate on the streets is ten times as high as for people who live inside," Mac said.

"So they either move away or die, is that what you're saying?"

"Or they get off the streets."

"That's what I was getting at. Some do get off the streets, right?"

"Some. The lucky few."

"Few ... so it's not a lot."

"Not as many as I'd hope but it does happen."

"And you've seen it, right?"

He nodded his head. "I've seen it. Heck, I've been it."

"What do you mean?" I asked.

"Where did you think I lived before I started working here?" Mac asked.

"You lived on the streets?"

"Streets, alleys, dumpsters, hostels ... although to tell you the truth most of the time I was living inside a bottle."

"You were a ... a ..."

"A drunk. Although now I guess I'd call myself an alcoholic."

"But you don't drink now, do you?"

"Not any more. Haven't for more than a decade but I'm still an alcoholic. Once an alcoholic always an alcoholic."

"What made you stop?" I asked.

"I woke up one morning, face down in the gutter. Beside me was my best buddy, a guy I'd been drinking with for a long time. I gave him a shake, trying to wake him, but he wouldn't wake up. He couldn't wake up. Dead. I knew right then that I had a choice. It was either stop drinking or stop living. I decided it was time to try ... and I did."

Somehow none of this was really a surprise—I'd had my suspicions. Strange, though, it didn't make me think less of Mac ... maybe more. To fall down was one thing, but to pull yourself back up again, that took something ... something special.

"So you just stopped."

"It's a little more complicated than that."

"So what did you do? How did you do it?"

"For starters I went to a detox."

"I've heard about them, but I don't really know what they're all about," I said.

"It's a place where people can be to go through the symptoms of withdrawal."

"There are withdrawal symptoms when you stop drinking?" I asked.

Mac laughed. "Shoot, I can laugh about it now, but there sure are symptoms. For me it was being violently ill, shaking, and feeling like my whole body was on fire. For others it's worse."

"How much worse can it get than that?"

"Hallucinations, paranoia, seizures."

"And these places, these detox centres, is it hard to get into one?"

"Not if you know the right people."

"And you know those people?"

"I could arrange a detox bed in a day or two," Mac said. "But a detox is just step one. You're there for ten to fourteen days. Enough time to allow the poison to leach out of your body. From there you go into a treatment facility. That could last at least a month, sometimes two, sometimes longer. And from there you have to get hooked into an after-care program ... something like Alcoholics Anonymous."

"I know about that—at least I've heard about it from the movies. You know, *my name is So-and-So and I'm an alcoholic*."

"There's a little more to it than that, but acknowledging you're an alcoholic is a pretty important first step along the path."

"Do you go to those meetings?" I asked.

"Three times a week. It works." Mac got a thoughtful look. "Is this a sort of general question or do you have somebody in mind?"

"Jack."

"Figured that."

"I thought you might have," I said. "I'm going to talk to him. Could you get him into a detox?"

"If he wanted," Mac said. "Did he tell you he wanted to stop drinking?"

"No ... not really."

"You ever heard the expression you can lead a horse to water but you can't make it drink?"

"What has that got to do with anything?" I asked.

"It means that just because you make it available to them doesn't mean they'll use it, take it, or appreciate it. If Jack wants detox I can arrange it. If he doesn't want it there's no *point* in arranging it."

"But there'd be no harm in me asking him if he wants it," I said.

"No harm. Just be prepared for what he might answer. When you goin' to talk to him?"

"I was hoping for tonight ... if he shows up ... but it sounds like he won't. Maybe I should go and find him."

"The park isn't the best place to be ... especially once it's dark."

"If I left right now it wouldn't be dark," I said.

"You tryin' to help Jack or just get out of work?"

"Maybe both."

"That gets me thinkin'. You've been here an awful lot lately."

"Are you getting tired of seeing me around?" I asked.

"Just figured you must be getting pretty close to the end of your hours here."

"Pretty close."

"How close?" Mac asked.

I smiled. "After tonight, one more hour."

"One more hour! Were you figuring on just finishing up and disappearing?"

"No. I was figuring on finishing up my hours and still showing up to help."

"Why would you be wanting to do that for?"

"It's certainly not because I want to see your smiling face. Is there any law that says I can't keep coming down here and helping just because I want to?"

"Only law in here is me," Mac said. "Let me look into your eyes," he said and spun me around so we were eye to eye. What was he doing?

"Yep, I can see it."

"See what?" I asked.

"Right there in your eyes. You're high."

"High? I'm not high!" I couldn't believe he was saying that to me.

"You're becoming addicted."

"I'm not, honest. I've never had more than two beers and that was at my cousin's wedding last December!"

"I'm not talking about alcohol and I'm not talking about drugs."

"What else is there?" I was completely lost. What was he talking about?

"You're high on helping."

"What?"

He smiled. "There's something about helping that makes you feel good. I can't figure out if it's the most selfish or selfless thing you can do. And once you start doing it you want to keep on doing it. That's why you want to keep coming back."

"And can I?"

"You come down here any time you want, kid, any time." He put a hand on my shoulder. "I sort of thought from the beginning that you weren't just putting in hours."

"Then you thought wrong. All I wanted to do was get through and get out."

"Maybe the first couple of times but not after that," Mac said. "Look, I got too much respect for you to—"

"Respect for me?" I asked, surprised and shocked.

"Yeah, respect for you. Too much respect to be telling you what to do but I'm not so sure it's the smartest thing to be goin' down to the park right now."

"I'll be careful."

"It's not just that. You know, you gotta talk to somebody about their drinking at the right time. They say you gotta wait until an alcoholic hits rock bottom."

"How much lower can he get than sleeping in a tent and eating from dumpsters?" I asked.

"You'd be surprised. It also doesn't work if he's had so much to drink that he can't make sense of what you're saying. Understand?"

"I guess that makes sense."

"Good. Now if you're determined this is what you have to do, then you better get goin' before it gets dark."

"Thanks, Mac. I'll let you know what happens. See you tomorrow."

Sixteen

I ENTERED THE PARK. It was still light. That was good. I also knew exactly how to find the tents. That was even better. I just hoped that Jack was going to be there—be there and sober enough to talk to me. As I walked I looked continually around me. Nobody was going to sneak up on me. Up my left sleeve was the metal bar. I'd brought it with me just in case. I'd rather run, though, if I had a choice. I really didn't know if I could use it.

I skipped off the path and onto the little dirt trail. I moved as fast as I could, careful for the roots and rocks in the ground and the branches blocking the way. Soon the little fire was visible through the trees before the tents could be seen. I entered the clearing and saw Jack immediately. He was sitting in one of the canvas chairs. There was nobody else to be seen. I yelled out a greeting. He didn't move or react. Maybe he hadn't heard me.

"Hey, Jack," I said as I stopped beside him. His eyes were closed, his head slumped over to one side, slightly snoring. He was asleep—or passed out.

"Jack?" I called a little louder. Still, no response. There was an empty bottle at his feet and he smelled of alcohol. He wasn't just asleep. Maybe I should just leave. Maybe I shouldn't.

I gave him a little shake. "Hey, Jack, it's me … Ian!"

He roused and his eyes popped open. With heavy eyelids he looked up at me. At first there was only a dull glare, like he didn't even know me, then his eyes cleared and he smiled.

"Hey, Ian, how are you doing?" His words were slurred. It was obvious that he was drunk.

"I'm good. You?"

"Fine. I must have fallen asleep."

"I'm sorry I woke you up," I said, although obviously not that sorry or I wouldn't have done it.

"That's okay." He stretched. "You know, I've been thinking about Rwanda a lot lately."

"Me too."

"Most of the time over the last few years I've tried hard *not* to think about it," he said.

"I didn't mean to dredge up bad memories for you," I apologized.

He shrugged. "Some things are better talked about. It wasn't like I'd forgotten about it … it's not like I'll ever forget about it."

"It's just that I didn't know how really awful it was."

He scowled. "You *still* don't know how awful it was. Nobody who wasn't there could ever know."

"Of course … I didn't mean anything … of course I don't really know."

He reached up and patted my hand. "I shouldn't have snapped like that. You're a good boy." He shook his head and smiled. "Been remembering lots of things … thinking about being a kid … about my mother and father. My mother used to say to me, Jacques, you have to know—"

"Jacques? I thought your name was Jack?" I said, cutting him off.

"Jack is what they call me around here. Jacques is what my parents named me."

"I didn't know that ... What should I call you?"

He didn't answer right away. "Jacques would be fine. It would be nice to hear my name said sometimes. It would remind me of who I was ... once ... a long time ago."

"Sure, Jacques."

He smiled. "You said that with a little French accent. Do you speak any French?"

"Just grade ten high school French. Enough to order a pizza, find a washroom, or read a sign or directions. So you're French?"

"French *Canadian*. Both parts are important. Both parts are to be proud of."

His eyes closed and he stopped talking. I wasn't sure if he was thinking or if he'd passed out.

"Jacques?"

"Yeah?"

"You were saying you were proud of being Canadian and French."

He nodded in agreement. "I am. You know, one of the reasons I was assigned to Rwanda was because I spoke French."

"That's right, that's one of the official languages, along with English and ... and ..."

"And Kinyarwanda. It's not good just to speak one language."

"I speak some Spanish," I said.

"How is it that you can speak Spanish?"

"I don't really speak it as much as I understand it. I learned it from Berta. She was my nanny when I was little and now she is our housekeeper ... but really she's more than that. She's from Guatemala."

"Guatemala is a beautiful country. I guess she could probably tell you stories about the things that go on there."

"She's told me stories about growing up," I said.

"Has she told you stories about the disappeared?"

I shook my head. What was he talking about?

"Not surprised she hasn't. Who wants to talk of those things?"

I didn't know what he meant. "So you were telling me about something your mother told you."

"Yeah, that's right. My mother would say to me, Jacques, the world is nothing but a battle between God and the Devil, between good and evil. A constant battle. In Rwanda I saw evil win the battle."

Jack, I mean *Jacques,* got up from the chair. He struggled to get to his feet and staggered. For a second I thought he was going to tumble over backwards before he regained his balance.

"You see that jacket?" he said, pointing to a coat lying on the ground beside one of the tents.

"Yeah." That was a strange question.

"When I see it do you know what I think? I think it's a body. I can't see a shirt or even a rag lying there without thinking there's a body underneath. Did you notice where they had piled up branches by the playground, branches they'd pruned from dead trees?"

"No," I said, shaking my head.

"When I see them I don't see branches, I see limbs … human limbs … I see arms and legs, cut off and stacked like firewood because that's what I've seen. Those are memories that are seared into my mind."

"I'm so sorry. I didn't mean to bring all that back."

"You didn't bring it back because it never went away," he said. "It won't ever go away, no matter how hard I try to forget, no matter what I do or think … but maybe that's right. *Somebody* has to remember. Somebody has to grieve for the loss. Somebody."

It was then that I noticed that he was crying. Tears were freely flowing down his cheeks. I wanted to say something, do something, put my arm around him, but I just stood there feeling awkward and stupid and helpless.

"And do you know what the worst part of the whole thing was?" he asked.

I couldn't even imagine which part from all the others could be the worst.

"None of it had to happen. We could have stopped it, we saw it coming, and they wouldn't listen."

"Who ... who wouldn't listen?" I was struggling to form words.

"The United Nations. They sent us to perform a mission and then wouldn't let us do what was needed. They wouldn't give us the men or the equipment, or the permission to do what we *knew* had to be done." He wiped the tears away with the back of a dirty sleeve. "Just a few hundred more men, more ammunition for our guns, permission to seize the arms we knew were being built up that were eventually used in the genocide, a plane to jam the radio signals of that station that was spewing out hate and violence, the orders to capture the key men—the *devils*—who orchestrated the massacres. All of this could have been done, was within our reach, but they would not let us. And do you know why?"

I shook my head ever so slightly. Not only didn't I have an answer I was so transfixed that I could hardly budge.

"Racism," he said, the word hardly audible. "This genocide was an act of complete and utter racism."

"But ... but you said that the groups, the two main groups, were both black, were almost the same," I said.

"The racism did not involve them. It involved *us*. The United Nations knew what was going on. The United States, Great Britain, France, Russia, Canada. We all knew, but we did not step in. Who cares if a bunch of savages, a faceless mass of ignorant blacks, get killed? So what? It's just less of them to die of starvation, or AIDS, or some other disease! Less of them to have to feed and take care of! Who cares?" he yelled and his face was a mask of anger and hatred. I stepped back. "We stood there, helpless ... no, worse than helpless. We stood by and were witness to the atrocities we couldn't stop."

He picked up a stick and poked the embers of the fire. I knew his actions had less to do with tending to the flames and more to do with trying to compose himself.

"All that is required for evil to prevail is for good men to do nothing," Jacques said.

"What?"

"Edmund Burke. For evil to triumph all that is required is for good men to do nothing. In Rwanda I served with some of the best, most noble men I have ever been privileged to know. We tried to do something. We wanted to do something. We were not allowed. Even worse, we were not even allowed to turn away. We were forced to watch. Watch as churches turned from places of sanctuary to scenes of carnage, watch as streets became painted red with blood, where the bodies were so many that they were carried away in dump trucks, where torn and tattered human beings were left to die on corners or in fields, where the hospitals couldn't hope to help the masses that were brought there. I have seen so much ... so very much ..."

He started to cry again. He looked up at me. "You have to know that we tried ... we really tried."

"I know you did. You did everything you could do."

"We provided sanctuary, places where we could protect some people. We arranged convoys where people could be taken through the lines to safety. We went out every day and saved some people from mobs, supervised those convoys, putting our lives in the middle, willing to lay down our lives to save those people. We couldn't stop it ... but we slowed it down ... just a little."

He started to cry even harder. "You have to know that we tried ... we really tried." He choked out the words between the sobs.

"I know you did. You did everything you could do."

His entire body shook violently like he was going to become physically sick. He took a deep breath. "We did our best."

"I know you did."

"You know, I wouldn't blame you if you didn't believe me. Sometimes *I* have trouble believing it. I think back to all the things we did, the things we didn't do, the things we could have done, or should have done, or might have done. I try to remember the lives that were saved—that *we* saved. Instead all I can remember is the victims. The countless number of victims."

"They became statistics," I said, recalling my teacher's words—the words of Joseph Stalin ... Joseph Stalin, the mass murderer.

"I try to understand the numbers," Jacques said. "I think about 9/11, about the planes crashing into the twin towers. What a tragedy."

I nodded my head. "I still think about that some times." My parents both worked in office buildings, and the images of those planes crashing into the buildings and then the towers tumbling down was so clear in my mind.

"Think about that happening and then the next day two more planes crashing into two more towers. And then it happened the next day, and the next and the next. But it didn't just happen for a week. It happened every day for 265 days in a row. If you can imagine that then you can imagine the number of people that were killed in Rwanda."

"That's ... that's almost impossible to comprehend."

"It is. And for us, in Rwanda, it was like watching the planes crashing and going to the airport and telling them not to let any more planes leave, but nobody listened to us and two more planes took off and crashed. And we went back to warn them and another two planes took off, and two more the next day, and the next ..." He let his sentence trail off.

I stood there too stunned and scared and confused to know what to say or even if I *should* try to say something. Standing in front of me was this man—this big man, this man who had been so strong, so powerful, so noble, and now was just this, and I knew why he had become what he had become. He was just another victim of Rwanda.

Seventeen

I SAT BOLT UPRIGHT in bed, fighting the urge to scream out ... It was just a dream ... just a nightmare. My body shuddered and I struggled to slow down my racing heart. It had seemed so real ... no ... so *surreal*. Those three thugs had been chasing me through the park, waving machetes at me, trying to cut off my limbs. And I ran and I ran to try and get away from them, but I couldn't lose them. And as I ran there were bodies and blood, torn limbs piled like firewood. And there among the bodies was Jacob, those soft brown eyes staring up at me, silently pleading with me to save him, but who was going to save me? And then there was Jacques. His words, his voice, the things he'd said to me. It was all so awful.

Why had I gone to speak to him? Why hadn't I just left well enough alone? There was nothing for me to gain in knowing any of this. I was better off before. It wasn't like knowing changed anything. It didn't make anything better for anybody else. It just made it worse for me.

There was no point in even pretending I was going to be able to go to sleep. I threw off the covers and climbed out of bed. I'd left my computer on and the screen saver swirled out a pattern of light that led me across my room. I opened the door. My way was now lit by the little night light glowing from downstairs. Quietly, so as not to disturb anybody, I went down the stairs. I started for the kitchen, stopped, and then turned around and went to the front door. I wanted to make sure it was locked. I jiggled the handle. It was locked. I headed back for the kitchen, flicking on the light. I opened the fridge and pulled out the milk pitcher.

"Can't sleep?"

I jumped into the air, spun around, and almost dropped the milk. It was Berta.

"I didn't mean to scare you," she said.

"I wasn't scared. Just startled." This certainly hadn't made my heart beat any slower. "I tried to be quiet. Did I wake you?"

"You know me, I hear sounds even when there are no sounds."

"Would you like a glass of milk too?" I asked, holding up the pitcher.

"Warm milk would be nice."

"Ughhh!"

"Warm, *chocolate* milk," Berta said. She opened up a cupboard and pulled out a big container of hot chocolate. "Well?"

"That would be okay."

She filled the kettle with water and put it on the stove while I grabbed two mugs and put them on the table.

"So what's stopping *carino mio* from sleeping?"

"Too many thoughts."

"What thoughts?"

"About people ... about the way people treat each other."

"Most people treat each other well," Berta said.

"And others treat them like they're nothing ... less than nothing ... There's an evil at work."

"Evil is a strong word."

"What other word would you use to describe the Holocaust, the killing fields of Cambodia, the genocide in Rwanda?"

"Those responsible for the disappeared in Guatemala," Berta said softly.

I looked up at her. She had turned away. She was standing, staring at the kettle, waiting for it to boil.

"Berta?" I asked.

She kept staring at the kettle.

"My friend, the soldier, the homeless man, he said something to me about the disappeared. He said you'd know about them."

"I know." Again the words were so soft. She was still looking away.

"Berta … you don't have to tell me anything … we can just have our hot chocolate." To be honest I didn't know if I was trying to protect her or myself.

The kettle started to whistle and she took it off the burner. I put two heaping spoonfuls of the hot chocolate powder into each cup and Berta poured in the boiling water. The tinkling of the spoons against the mugs was the only sound. Berta sat down at the table, opposite me.

"The things I could say would not help either of us sleep," she said.

"I don't think I'm going to be sleeping much either way."

"Me neither." She dipped her spoon into her drink, blew on it, and sampled a little bit. "There are things I don't talk about."

"You don't have to talk about it." I was feeling like I'd heard too much already.

"I don't have to talk. I don't want to talk. Maybe it is time that I *should* talk. Maybe it is not too soon any more." She blew on her hot chocolate. "What do you know about Guatemala?"

"I know some things. Of course I know it's where you're from. It's in Central America. It's by the equator and hot. It's poor. I know that you're supporting half the children in the country."

Berta laughed. "I'm helping to support seven children."

Berta had seven foster children that she sponsored by making monthly donations to an orphanage in Guatemala. I knew my parents paid her pretty well, but that was still a lot of money to send away every month—not that she'd ever complain. I also knew if my parents did pay her more she'd probably just support another child in the orphanage.

"Don't you also send them extra money all the time for the other kids in the orphanage?" I asked.

"Occasionally ... Christmas ... Easter ... when they need some extra help." She took a sip from her hot chocolate. "Your parents made a very generous contribution last Christmas."

"They did?"

"I think they didn't want to make a deal of it ... Maybe I shouldn't have even mentioned it," she said.

I was a little surprised ... but then again, what was a few dollars or even a few *thousand* dollars to them? I wanted to change the subject, get it away from my parents.

"So with the extra donations there are more than seven children you take care of."

"More in some ways," she agreed. "Although I like to think I have eight children. The seven in Guatemala and one here." She reached across the table and patted my hand. I felt all tingly inside.

"I'll tell you some other things about my country that I don't talk about. For thirty-six years my country was in a civil war. You know what that means, *si?*"

"Of course. That's a war being fought by people within the same country."

"In a rich country a civil war would be terrible, but in a poor country it is devastating. People who had so little to begin with ended up with nothing. Villages destroyed, fields burning or abandoned.

Those who were just barely surviving before couldn't survive any more."

"Who was the fighting between?" I asked.

"The government, which wanted to keep control and wealth away from the people, and those who wanted a say in running the country. Many of those were the people who lived on the land, the peasants, the native peoples. People fled from the conflict. Over one million people became refugees. Fleeing their homes, fleeing the country, searching for a safe place … but there were hardly any safe places."

"I can't even imagine losing my home."

"It is better than losing your life. There were also many, many deaths. It is thought that over one hundred thousand people were killed … disappeared."

"Disappeared." That was what Jacques called it. "What does that even mean?"

She shrugged. "Disappeared. The people were there at night, sleeping in their beds, but gone in the morning. Disappeared. That's when the death squads came … at night."

That was how it was for Jacob.

"That is when they came to my house," Berta said softly.

"Your house?" I gasped.

"To my house," she said. The words had been just barely audible. She looked up at me. "My father was a newspaper editor in Puerto Barrios. He wrote things that he believed in. Those beliefs cost him his life. And the life of my brother … and my mother."

I listened intently, not believing my ears—not wanting to believe my ears.

"It was at night when they came. I was sleeping. I heard the noise, the screaming, the yelling, and I scrambled out of my bed and into my closet—the way my father had told me I should. He always told me that we had nothing to fear but then he made me promise to go into the closet if I heard screaming. I hid underneath blankets and clothing on the floor of the closet. They looked—I heard the heavy boots stomping into my room, heard the furniture being overturned, heard the door of the closet being opened, but somehow, like a miracle, like God was protecting me, they did not see me."

I pictured it all in my mind—I could see it so clearly. It was like with Jacob, except they didn't find Berta. Thank God they hadn't found her.

"I lay there underneath the clothing, trembling, terrified, afraid to breathe or move. I lay there long after the noises had stopped and the voices had faded. I think I even fell asleep. I woke up and it was silent. I lay there for the longest time, listening, hardly daring to peek out from under the blankets. Then I saw a crack of light coming under the door and knew it was morning. I came out, afraid to even call out … afraid that somebody might hear me, but more afraid that when I called there would be nobody to hear me. My room was torn to pieces. Dolls that my grandmother had given me were smashed, the night table overturned, the bed where I had been asleep, the mattress, was slashed open with the stuffing bleeding out. That was what the whole house was like. Nothing taken, just smashed and destroyed, left behind for anybody to see as a warning of what could happen. And, of course, my family was gone. Disappeared."

She paused and looked directly up at me. I expected to see tears, upset, anguish. Her face was a mask of calm. That was even more upsetting to me than if there had been tears.

"I never saw my family again, never even knew where they had gone or how they had died, but knew that they would never return."

"I didn't know," I said, the words barely able to form in my mouth.

"I never told you. I never even told your parents."

"How old were you?"

"The age you are going to be. Sixteen."

"And if those men had found you …?"

"I would have known the fate of my family because it would have been my fate too. I would have been killed. Tortured, raped, and then killed. That's when I knew I had to leave … before they came back."

"Where did you go?"

"First to a neighbour. The place my father had told me to go. From there he brought me to a man who lived in our village. He arranged for me to escape. First to Mexico and then to Canada. My father had, prepared it all, arranged it all. He knew what could happen."

"But if he knew, why didn't you all just leave *before* it happened?" I asked.

"My mother tried, many times, to convince him that we needed to go. He thought because he was an editor, because of the influence his family had, that we would be safe. He said it was his country and he couldn't just abandon it. He had to try to make changes for the good of his country, for the good of his family."

"But it didn't do anybody any good."

"In the long run, who knows?" Berta said. "The things he believed in, that he spoke out for, that he wrote about eventually became real. The death squads are now gone."

"But so is your family. Was it worth it?" I could scarcely bear to ask her this, but I had to know.

"My father thought it was. Democracy is now alive in Guatemala."

"I just don't know how you could have gone on after what happened to your family. I don't think I could have been that strong."

"You would be surprised what you are capable of when you have no choice. Eon, you are very strong, very strong."

"I don't know."

"I do," she said. She reached over and took my hand in hers. "I know how strong you are, what is inside of you."

"I'm not that strong."

"No? Does it take strength to go down to that place and help those poor street people?"

"What I do is nothing."

"Not nothing to those people you help. Not nothing to me. You make me so proud."

This was all so strange. She was telling me about the terrible deaths of her family and she was the one comforting me.

"I guess I understand why it's so hard for you to get to sleep," I said.

She nodded. "Silly, after all these years they are still so vivid in my dreams ... in my nightmares." She paused. "Sometimes I think the only way to free myself from the thoughts is to go back home."

"Would that be safe?"

"It is now. There would be nothing to fear."

"And you think going back would help?"

"It could."

"Then why don't you try it?" I asked.

"Not yet. What would you do?"

"I'd be fine for a few weeks. I'm sure that ..." It suddenly dawned on me that she wasn't talking about a vacation. "You mean to go there and live?"

She nodded. I felt my whole body go hot and then cold.

"But not now ... someday."

A wave of relief washed over me.

"Instead I do what I can," she said. "I send money. I help in my small way."

"It's not a small way for those seven children."

"It is like I have read. It is better to light a candle than to curse the darkness. I have seven candles that I keep alight."

I reached out and took her other hand and held them both in mine. "Eight," I said.

Eighteen

I WALKED WITH A HESITATION in my step. I knew what I was going to say and do, I just didn't know exactly why I thought I should. I'd rehearsed the lines, but I was still wondering if I should say them. What right did I have? And even if I did have the right, did I have the guts to follow through? I'd spent the entire day in school thinking about those questions. Was Berta right? Was I strong ... was I strong enough?

I turned into the park. I'd keep an eye open for anything that could cause me grief, but if trouble found me, then I'd take care of it. The metal bar was up my sleeve. If I had to use it today I could—I would.

I was going to find Jacques and talk to him. I had things I needed to say. Things he needed to hear. I just had to find him. Find him alone and sober enough that he could listen to me. It was strange—ironic—that I wanted to talk to him about his drinking but I could only talk to him if he hadn't been drinking too much.

I was just going to take the cut-off to the tents when I saw Jacques. He was sitting on a bench. He had a cigarette in one hand and a brown paper bag in the other. He brought the bag up to his face—it was no big secret what was in the bag. I walked over until I was standing right beside him. He didn't seem to notice.

"Hello, Jacques," I said.

He looked up and seemed surprised by my presence. "Hey, Ian, good to see you!"

His words were slurred, his eyes glazed over. The smell of alcohol was incredibly strong.

"I was hoping to talk to you," I said.

"Talk away. You want a slug?" he asked, holding the bag out toward me.

"What?" I asked in shock, backing slightly away.

"You want a drink ... red wine," he said as he removed the bottle partway from the bag to show me the label. "Not the best, but the best four bucks can buy."

"I'm only fifteen," I said. "I'm too young to drink."

"Since I was about twelve my parents always let me have a little glass of wine over dinner," he said.

"I don't want to drink ... and I don't think you should be drinking either." My mouth felt dry—I really didn't know where this was going to go.

Jacques took another sip from the bottle.

"Did you hear what I said?" I asked.

He lowered the bottle. "I heard you." He raised the bottle again, this time tipping it back farther and longer and chugging down the wine.

I reached over to grab the bottle. "You shouldn't be doing that!" I said.

"And you shouldn't be doing that!" he snapped, shaking off my hand from the bottle. He staggered to his feet and started to walk away. I jumped up and chased after him.

"It's just that I think you should stop drinking," I said as I caught up and stopped right in front of him.

"I think you should leave me alone."

"I can't do that. I won't do that. Mac told me about places that can help you to stop drinking."

"I don't need help."

"Yes, you do. You could get into a detox centre and from there they could arrange for a treatment facility and—"

"I'm not going no place except to my tent." He started to walk away but I blocked his way.

"If you stopped drinking you wouldn't have to live in a tent. You could go home."

"Home?" he asked. "I haven't got any home."

"But you could."

"What do you really know about my life?" he demanded.

"I know it could be better than it is now." I wasn't going to let him scare me.

"You don't know nothing." He pushed past me.

"It doesn't matter what happened in Rwanda!" I shouted out. He stopped.

He staggered back a few feet toward me. "It *does* matter what happened," he snapped. "Maybe nobody else cares, maybe nobody else even remembers, but I remember and I will never ... *ever* forget."

"You can put it all behind you ... you can put your life back together again!"

Suddenly his arm came up and he tossed the bottle of wine at me! It whizzed by my head and there was the sound of smashing glass as it crashed against the path behind me! I leapt into the air, spinning around, my heart jumping into my throat!

"You tried to hit me!" I gasped.

"If I tried to hit you, I would have hit you. You see those shards of glass?" he said, pointing to the jagged pieces of the bottle on the ground. "Do you think you can put them together again? Do you think anything or anybody could ever make it whole again? Well, do you? It's not just broken, it's *shattered* into a million pieces and it can never be put back together again. Never. And even if you could, through some miracle, make it whole again, you'd *never* be able to recapture what was inside the bottle. It's gone, forever. That bottle … that's me … nobody, nothing, can ever put the pieces together again. And even if my life could be put back together again, it would never be the same. What was inside of me," he said, placing his hands on his chest, "that is gone … gone *forever*."

He walked away. I stood there, my mouth open, my mind empty.

Nineteen

"TIME TO WAKE UP!"

My eyes popped open. I was suddenly very awake. "Berta, what are you doing?"

"You don't want to be late."

"I guess I didn't set my alarm or I slept through it. If I get dressed real quick can you drive me to school?" My heart was pounding as I tried to come fully awake.

"There is no school!" Berta said. "It is Sunday."

"Sunday ... but why are you getting me up early on a Sunday?" I groaned.

"Because Sunday is the day when church is held."

"Sure, that's the day for church but what's that got to do with you getting me up?" I pulled the sheet up over my chin. "I know it isn't Christmas and I'm pretty sure it isn't Easter either, so I should be sleeping," I complained.

"You're allowed to go to church more than twice a year—there's no law," Berta said.

"Maybe not a law, but it's certainly a family tradition." I yawned. The more Berta was talking the more I was waking up. "I wonder what got into my parents?"

"Nothing. Your parents don't even know you're going to church. They're still asleep."

"There's no way I'm going to go on my own," I grumbled.

"Not on your own. With me."

That really woke me up. "Why would you take me to church?"

"Because we're going to *my* church."

"Your church? Isn't the service in Spanish?" I asked.

"There's a little bit of English. Besides you understand Spanish."

"Not enough to understand a whole church service," I argued.

"Who says anything about understanding? Because it's in Spanish that will make it even easier for you to drift off and ignore what is being preached."

"Come on, Berta, this doesn't make sense." I pulled my blanket over my head.

Suddenly the covers were ripped off and I was there on the mattress in my boxers, feeling exposed and practically naked.

"Berta!" I exclaimed. "I'm not dressed!"

"Get up and *get* dressed."

"Be reasonable," I pleaded. "Just give me one good reason why I should go to church with you this morning."

"Fine. How about because I want you to come?"

I didn't know how to argue with that. "Could you explain *why* you want me to come?"

"I would enjoy your company. Besides, there is somebody I want you to meet, to talk to."

"Couldn't we meet someplace else ... sometime later in the day?"

She shook her head. "Then and there. This man is leaving the country tomorrow morning. You need to meet him today and he will be at church."

"Can't I talk to him after church ... a lot after church? I don't want to go to your church. I'm not even Catholic."

"I'm not asking you to convert. I just need you to talk to him."

I could see how determined Berta was but I wasn't going to give up easily.

"Can't you have him come over to the house after church ... this afternoon or evening?"

"No good," she said. "He is very busy. A few minutes is all we could possibly get after church." She paused. "After that he goes back to Guatemala."

"He's from your country?"

"He is from my hometown."

"I still don't know why you want me to meet him."

"Isn't it enough to know that I want you to? Just do as I ask as a favour for me."

I didn't answer right away. What I wanted to say was that I'd do anything for Berta, but I was too embarrassed to say it. I knew, though, that I was going to be going.

"Can we at least have something to eat before we go?" I asked.

"I'll fix you something, something good. How about an omelette, with cheese and green peppers and onions and maybe a little ham?"

"How about a lot of ham?"

Berta bent down and gave me a kiss on the top of my head. "A lot of ham."

"Now, could I be left alone so I can get dressed?" I asked, trying to sound angry. "Unless you want me to go to church in my boxers."

"You dress as you wish, but remember, we are all naked before God."

"That might make for some interesting church services."

Berta started to giggle. "Get dressed and I will cook. Put on a suit— I want you to look good."

CHURCH WAS PRETTY MUCH THE SAME in Spanish as it was in English—boring. Although Berta was right, it was easier to ignore in a language I didn't understand. At first I struggled to pull down little bits of Spanish out of the air and try to link them together to make sense of things. I was actually amazed that I had got the basic idea of some of what was happening. Other parts of the service weren't that much different from our services—collection plates, hymns, shaking hands—I even recognized the Lord's Prayer even though it was in Spanish. After a while, though, it was just too tiring to try to keep up and I officially turned off my efforts.

I just wished I could turn my mind off that easily for other things. I'd spent more time thinking about Jacques ... about our last conversation and about his life. Even when I wasn't thinking about it, it was still there. It was just below the surface. I'd suddenly have a sense of being uneasy, of something being wrong, and then it would all come tumbling back into my brain. And when I was thinking about Jacques I was thinking about Rwanda ... and Cambodia, and Armenia, and Yugoslavia, and Nazi Germany, and those three thugs in the park.

I knew that last part was stupid, linking them with those terrible tragedies around the world but that was the closest thing to violence I'd ever experienced, and I couldn't help wondering—how much different were those three from those other monsters? If they had total power, what would they have done to me? I had no answers. I had no answers to any of it. Here I was sitting in a church, supposedly in the house of God, and all I could think about was the work of the devil. If God was everywhere, how come he hadn't shown up in Rwanda?

I guess all of those thoughts were what had made Berta bring me here today. I'd spent the last few days just moping around the house. I hadn't been sleeping very well and my appetite was really down. That was stupid. Not eating around Berta was like a scream for help. I knew

I could snap out of it. It could take a few days, a week at most. I didn't need to come to church or to meet anybody. I didn't want to talk to anybody. I just wanted to be left alone to wallow in the bad feelings until they finally went away.

The choir struck up another song and they started to file out of the choir loft and down the aisle toward the exit. I knew what that meant in any language. The altar boys and the two priests followed behind them and out the door and the service was over. Over and out the door. The people in the first pews were now coming down the aisle, closely followed by the people in the next pew and the next. I had a great view since I was the tallest person in the whole church ... by a long shot. I was head and shoulders taller. I'd also noticed that everybody was looking at me. It wasn't simply that I was a stranger, but a tall, non-Spanish-looking stranger.

"So what now?" I asked Berta.

"Now we talk to Eduardo."

"Who exactly is Eduardo?" I asked. On the way to church she hadn't said anything more about the man from her hometown—the man she so desperately wanted me to meet.

"He is here visiting from Guatemala. In my country he is very important. A very big hero."

"A hero ... where is he?" I asked, looking around the still-emptying church.

"He is already gone outside. He was sitting in the front row."

I hadn't noticed anybody who looked like a hero. We stood up and joined the people shuffling out of the church. Outside in the sunshine the crowd had fanned out but people were still standing around. It was like they were reluctant to get into their cars and leave. They stood around, laughing, talking in Spanish. That made everybody sound excited. Spanish always made me think that people were in a rush, the way the words just kept flooding out.

People kept coming up and greeting Berta and she introduced me to each of them—I was her *Eon*. And that was how almost everybody else said it too. *Eon*. Everybody was friendly and full of smiles and shook my hand or patted my arm. I was completely different from anybody else here but somehow I felt like I was welcome, almost like I belonged. My church hardly ever gave me that feeling.

"I know," I said quietly to Berta, "that I've been kind of preoccupied the last few days but I really don't need to talk to anybody."

"I don't want you to talk to him. I want you to listen to him."

"What's he going to say?" I asked.

"I do not know, but he always seems to know what to say."

"Sounds like you've known him for a long time."

"Since I was a child. He was the man who fixed the shoes in my town."

"He's a shoemaker? I thought you said he was a hero?" I asked.

"You can be both."

"But why do you want me talk to him?" I asked. It was strange enough when I thought she had wanted me to talk to a hero, but a shoemaker?

"He has things he can tell you about what happened in my country. About the death squads."

I was taken aback. This was just about the last thing I wanted to hear anything about. Wasn't I having enough trouble sleeping as it was?

"Maybe I don't want to know any more," I said.

"I thought that, then I decided I was wrong ... and so are you. You need to know more."

"What's the point?" I asked. "Knowing what happened doesn't change what happened."

"You're right. You can't change what happened. Maybe, though, it can help you change what will happen in the future."

I snorted. "Do you really think there's anything I can do that can make that big a difference?"

"Little things make big differences sometimes. Come."

Berta took me by the hand and led me through the crowd. It seemed like she knew everybody we passed. Still more greetings. Lots of hugs. Lots of smiles. This seemed more like a festival than a church.

"There he is," she said.

"Where?"

"In the group, in the centre of those women."

"In the centre ... you don't mean that man, do you?" I asked. There was a tiny old man, practically lost from view among the women. He was leaning heavily on a cane.

"*Si,* that is him."

"But, but, he's so old ... and small."

"Do you think somebody has to be big to be brave?" Berta asked.

"No, of course not. I just thought he'd be ... be different."

"He *is* different," she said.

We stood slightly off to the side while this little old man continued to be surrounded by people. Some left and others joined in and it looked like it could be a long time before we'd be able to talk to him. I really didn't want to be here. Maybe I could just wait in the car. Suddenly the man looked up and in our direction. His eyes widened in recognition as he saw Berta.

"Berta!" he yelled out. He moved forward surprisingly quickly, his cane tapping the pavement, and gave her a big hug and then reached up and kissed her on both cheeks. They talked in animated Spanish— is that saying the same thing twice?

"Eduardo," Berta said, "I would like to introduce you to a very special person. This is Eon."

"I'm most pleased to meet you," he said as we shook hands.

"I'm pleased to meet you, too."

"Berta has told me about you in our letters."

"You've written about me?" I asked.

"She mentions you all the time," he said.

"I just didn't know you did that."

"You know I send letters to the orphanage all the time," she said. "Eduardo runs the orphanage."

"Helps to run the orphanage," he said. "There are many people there, and here, who are part of the job."

"But I thought you repaired shoes?"

He smiled. "I still do that, but only for the children of the orphanage. We think it is important to take care of their soles as well as their souls." He turned directly to me. "But that is only because of the generosity of people such as Berta ... She has given so much ... has provided so much to our children. I just wish more people could be so generous of spirit. She is a very special person ... a very caring soul."

"You don't have to tell me that," I said.

Berta looked like she was blushing. "Do you know who Eduardo is?" Berta asked.

"Sure. You just told me—he runs the orphanage."

"He is also the man who saved my life."

My eyes widened in shock. This little man ... this little old man, leaning on his cane ... he was the man?

"You give me too much credit. I was one of many, many people who worked together to bring people out of Guatemala."

"He always downplays what he did," Berta said.

"Nonsense," he said. "I simply did what was right. What choice was there?"

"You could have done nothing," she said. "Instead you risked your life."

"I was not concerned. Who thinks that a simple shoemaker could be doing anything of consequence? I was too small a fish for the sharks to notice."

A chill went up my spine. I knew he was talking about the death squads, about those who did the killing, who made people disappear.

"What are you doing up here now?" I asked, needing to redirect the conversation away from an area I didn't want to talk about.

"Visiting," he said as he reached out and gave Berta's hand a squeeze. He looked around. "There are so many here that I know ... so many. I just wish that it could have been more ... that more could have been saved."

I felt a jolt of electricity surge through my body—those were almost exactly the same words that had come out of Jacques' mouth. I looked at him—right at him—right into his eyes. He'd seen some of the same things that Jacques had witnessed. He was half his size, spoke with a different accent, was a shoemaker and not a soldier, and didn't look anything like him, but there was something about this man that was the same as the other.

"You did all that you could," Berta reassured him.

"I know," he said, sadly nodding his head. "I know that now, but for years I only grieved over the ones who were lost. I could not get beyond the sadness for those who were killed."

"But you did get past it ... right?" I asked.

A soft, gentle smile came to his face—he looked serene, peaceful. "I have."

"How ... how did you get past it?" I asked, the words just a whisper as they escaped my lips.

"Many things in many ways."

"Could you tell me what they were?"

A thoughtful look came to his face. "Why is this of such interest to you?"

"It just is ... I have a friend ... I just want to know. Please."

He nodded his head. "It sounds like you are trying to help your friend but don't know how."

How did he know that? I looked over at Berta.

"I did not tell him," she said.

"There was no need to tell," Eduardo said. "I already knew. I will tell you. Time was one important thing," he said. "I needed time to think, to distance myself from the memories."

"So it's just a matter of time?" I asked.

"Time is necessary but not sufficient. You need more than just the passing of the days. Perhaps most important was helping others. It is a gift to the giver to help others. And, of course, I never lost my faith, and God's love. And then there was this ... this ... this will sound strange ... there was this man ... this beggar on the streets of Puerto Barrios. He told me a story."

"A story?"

"Yes. Would you like to hear it?"

I nodded my head.

"There was this man and he was walking along the beach ..."

Twenty

"I HAVE TO GO ... right now," I said.

"Now? But I thought we could stay and visit some more," Berta said.

"Yes, that would be most enjoyable," Eduardo agreed. "There is a little gathering in the courtyard behind the church."

"It is for Eduardo, for the orphanage, to raise funds."

"And to visit with many people I have known for so long. Please join us. You could have a typical meal from our homeland."

"I'd really like to stay, but I can't. I have to get going." I turned to Berta. "You can stay, Berta. I can get there by myself."

"Get where?" she asked. She sounded anxious and concerned.

"To the park."

She took a deep breath. "I will drive you."

"You've done enough. I have to do this on my own." I turned to Eduardo. I reached out my hand and shook his. "Thank you, sir, for what you did for Berta, for all those people. And thank you for the story."

He held on to my hand and looked directly at me ... no, it was like he was looking *inside* of me.

"I can see it in your eyes. You really do have something you have to do … I can see it … I can *feel* it," he said.

I felt uneasy, almost embarrassed, but somehow reassured.

Two women rushed over and barged into the conversation. Eduardo let go of my hand. He threw a burst of words at them, and the two women suddenly looked sheepish and went away as quickly as they had come.

I looked at Berta for explanation.

"They told Eduardo he had to come right away, that it wasn't right for the guest of honour not to be there at the meal," she said.

"And I told them I was in the middle of an important conversation and that I would hit them both on the backside with my cane if they didn't leave me alone!" he said sternly, but his eyes were twinkling.

I burst out laughing.

"One of the few benefits of growing as old as I have is that I can say what I want," he said. "Eon, I don't know where you are going or what you are needing to do, but I know you will do your best. Go … and may God go with you."

"Thanks."

"Eon, let me drive, let me help you," Berta said.

"I can do it on my own," I replied.

"I know you can, but is it not better to do it with help?" she asked.

"We all need help," Eduardo said. "Even those that do the helping."

"Thanks," I said. "I'd appreciate a ride."

BERTA HAD GIVEN ME a big hug, kisses on both cheeks, and then another hug, this one so long that I didn't think she was going to let go. Part of me didn't want her to let go. She drove away, leaving me on the sidewalk in front of the park.

I walked along the sidewalk, around the edge of the park, eyeing it as I walked. The park was alive with activity. There were parents out strolling with their kids and pushing carriages. The playground was filled with swinging, screaming, laughing children. The sound of birds could be heard above the noise of the traffic.

It was a bright, beautiful, sunny morning. So much different from the first time I'd walked through this park. Trees were in bloom, the grass was becoming a newer, truer shade of green, and flowers had pushed their way through the soil. New life. New beginnings. I knew why I'd come here. I knew what I wanted to say—what I needed to say. I just didn't know if I could make the words come out right, and even if I could it might not make any difference anyway. All I really knew was that if I didn't try, I'd regret it my entire life. Maybe I was doing this as much for myself as I was for him.

I started moving quickly. I wanted to get there before my nerve ran out. I jogged along the path and onto the dirt trail. I wished I was in my running shoes and sweats instead of a suit. Even more I wished that the suit had a metal bar up the sleeve. I dodged around the rocks and dipped under the overhanging branches. I slowed down and then stopped completely just before passing the last bushes that ringed the clearing. It was strange how this little line of bushes and trees divided two worlds. On one side, no more than fifty metres away, were parents and children playing, oblivious to what was just past this division. Maybe they wanted to be oblivious. That was something I could never be again. I took a deep breath and stepped through the divide.

I jogged along the path and immediately saw Jacques, sitting in what I'd come to think of as his canvas chair. He saw me and waved. Obviously he was awake—and probably sober—or at least had sobered up enough from whatever he'd drunk last night.

"Good morning!" he called out.

"Almost afternoon."

"No watch." He motioned for me to sit down and I did.

"Glad you came back. Afraid I'd chased you away with some of the things I said. That alcohol makes me like that sometimes." He paused. "I shouldn't drink so much."

"Yeah."

"I guess that was what you were trying to say to me."

"Trying to." I bit my tongue. There was no point in rubbing that part in. I needed to say some other things.

"You know I wasn't trying to hit you with that bottle," he said.

"It came pretty close."

"Closer than I meant, I've got to admit. I just didn't have the words to say what I was trying to say … my head was all foggy and it just sort of happened."

"That's okay," I said.

"I was just trying to explain things," he said, "make a point." We sat in silence for a few moments.

"You're dressed pretty fancy this morning," Jacques finally said.

"Just came back from church."

"Been a long time since I've been to church. Glad you came here afterwards to see me. I wanted to talk to you, to explain things, before I left."

"Left? Where are you going?"

"The West Coast. Ever been out there?"

"No, but I hear it's really nice. There's only one problem," I said. "No matter where you go, there'll you be."

"What?" Jacques asked.

"No matter where you go, no matter how far you run, you can't run away from yourself."

"Nobody's running," Jacques said. "Just time for a new place. Weather's better out there."

"Weather is better for living outside," I agreed. "But you're still running. The way you ran away from Rwanda."

"I never ran in Rwanda ... never!" he yelled as he leapt to his feet.

I gripped the arms of my chair to stop myself from jumping up and running away myself. I had to be calm. I didn't come here to get him angry at me. I took a deep breath before going on.

"I didn't say you ran in Rwanda. You didn't start running until you left Rwanda. After you got back home you started running and you never stopped."

He didn't answer. He just turned away.

"I'm not going to lie to you and tell you I know what it was like for you," I said. "Nobody could know who wasn't there, living it with you, seeing what you saw. I know that."

He turned around. "If you know that, you should know that I will never be able to forget those scenes, those faces, those people that I failed. Their blood is on my hands," he said, holding them out. "And they will never be clean again."

"You tried your best."

"Tried and failed."

"Tried and failed to save everybody, but you did save some ... right?"

"Not some," he said defiantly. "Thousands ... many thousands. We transported thousands to safety, allowed others to escape, provided sanctuary. We couldn't stop the death machine, but we got in its way, we slowed it down." His whole body shuddered and then he slumped back into his chair.

"I know what you're trying to do, Ian. And I thank you ... I really do. When I came back from Rwanda I tried to put it all away. I was trained as a soldier. Soldiers see things. They are trained to be strong, not to cry, not to let their feelings overwhelm them." He shook his head. "I tried to put it all behind me. I came back, I tried to get on with life, tried to be a good soldier ... maybe even a better soldier to make up for what I hadn't been able to do." He shook his head again slowly. "I couldn't do it. I couldn't get rid of the memories. That psychiatrist called it post-traumatic stress disorder. I call it not being able to be a soldier any more. They put me out to pasture, gave me a medical discharge. I tried, but I just couldn't forget."

"It would be impossible to forget. What you have to do is *remember*."

He looked up at me with an expression of confusion.

"To remember that you were just one human being trying to do his best. To remember that you *did* make a difference, that you *did* save lives. That you saved those lives by putting your own life at risk."

"I would have given up my life in a second. You know, there were men we had to send home because they stopped caring for their own safety completely. It was like they had seen so much that they didn't care if they were alive or dead any more."

"Is that what you're doing right now?" I asked. "Sacrificing your life to make up for the people you didn't save?"

"What?"

"Are you trying to give up your own life? Is that why you live like this?"

"You don't understand."

"I understand that you're not a hypocrite. I understand that you're not a coward. You're a man of honour. What I don't understand is that if every life is important then why isn't your life important?"

"My life is over."

"Only if you let it. Can I tell you a story?" I asked.

He raised his eyebrows in surprise. This wasn't what he'd expected, but like me, he couldn't resist hearing. "If you want to tell me a story, then I'll hear it. I've got no appointments that are pressing me."

I cleared my throat. "There's this man and he's walking along the beach, along a deserted section of the ocean. And as he rounds this point he sees in front of him an unbelievable scene. There on the beach, spread out across the sand, are starfish, thousands and thousands, maybe millions of starfish. They extend along the beach as far as the eye can see. The man stands there, stunned, hardly able to believe this scene before him. He wondered what caused this to happen, this massive tragedy. All of these starfish, up on the beach, out of the water, slowly dying."

I took a deep breath. "And as he's watching his eye is caught by the sight of motion farther along the beach. It's a person. Carefully he threads his way between the starfish, walking toward this other person. As he gets closer he realizes that it's a young boy. He can't be more than ten or eleven years old. As he walks he watches the boy. At first he doesn't know what the boy is doing, but then he realizes what he's seeing. The little boy is picking up starfish, one at a time, plucking them off the beach and tossing them back into the water.

"The man calls out to the boy. The boy waves back but continues to toss in starfish. The man talks to the boy about this scene that surrounds them, about the mysterious forces of nature. The boy keeps working. Taking another starfish and then another and throwing them back into the sea.

"'You know, son, what you're doing is very nice,' the man says, 'but look around. There are millions and millions of these starfish. What you're doing, it doesn't make a difference.'

"The boy picks up another starfish, tosses it into the water and then turns to the man. 'It made a difference for that one.' He picks up another starfish. 'And that one.' And picks up another starfish. 'And that one.'"

I looked up at Jacques. He was staring off into the distance. Silent, solemn, no expression betraying what was going on inside his head.

"Nobody is asking you to forget," I said. "I'm asking you to remember those that you saved and to honour those you couldn't save. Giving up your life honours nobody, saves nobody. By living like this you're saying that life isn't precious. It *is* precious. Every life ... including yours. Don't let Rwanda—don't let *evil*—claim one more victim. Don't let yourself be another casualty of Rwanda."

Jacques didn't answer. He sat there, silently, and a single tear rolled down his cheek.

"Pretty smart for a kid, aren't you?"

"I listen to smart people. I'm just hoping one smart person will listen to me."

"Been a long time since anybody called me smart."

"Maybe it's been a while since you did anything that was that smart. Maybe this is the time."

"Do you know how hard it is to pull yourself up from the bottom?" he asked.

"I don't know. I hope I'll never need to know. What I do know is that I believe in you. I believe that you're strong enough to make it back."

"I'm not that strong … not any more," he said.

"Nobody can make it on their own. I'm offering my help." I reached out my hand. "Come on, let's go and talk to Mac."

"Right now?"

"Right now."

He reached up and took my hand and I helped him to his feet.

"There's one other thing," I said. "Your father was wrong."

"My father? Wrong about what?"

"You said to me that he once told you that nobody ever thanks a soldier." I paused. "I want to thank you … for what you tried to do and what you did do. Thank you."

Twenty-One

"You almost finished out there?" Mac yelled as he poked his head out of the kitchen.

"Almost," I said as I continued to sweep.

"I swear you're getting slower and slower."

"You want more speed, you pay me more money."

"You're already getting paid twice as much as you're worth!" he taunted me.

"With that sort of attitude you're lucky I don't just quit!"

"The way you work you're lucky I don't just fire you!" he yelled back playfully. "Now put the broom down. I need you in the kitchen." He disappeared back into the kitchen.

I leaned the broom against the wall and walked toward the kitchen. We still had thirty minutes until the supper serving started so we had plenty of time to get things ready.

This was my third shift this week. Since school had ended I'd been putting in a lot of time—I had a lot of time to give. It was better to be here than just rattling around the house by myself. The place seemed awfully empty since—

"You coming or what?" Mac yelled through the door.

"I'm coming, I'm coming … keep your shirt on!" I pushed through the swinging door. "So what's the big emergency?"

"No emergency," Mac said, his smile dissolving into a wrinkly grin. "More like a celebration."

He stepped aside. There on the counter was a chocolate cake. On the top were two lit candles—a "1" and a "6."

"Happy birthday!" he yelled.

"You shouldn't have."

"Of course I should have. Now blow out the candles … and try not to spit on the cake, okay?"

"I'll try my best." I stood over top of the cake. In white frosting, it read Happy Birthday. I took a deep breath and—

"Wait!" Mac yelled, holding up his hands. "Did you make a wish?"

"No."

"Then you better."

"I don't believe in things like that," I said.

"What you got to lose? If you don't make a wish, you can't make it come true."

I thought of a half-dozen things I could have wished or wanted, but the only one that was important was Berta. I knew what I wanted. I wanted her to be safe and happy and enjoy her time away … and come back when that time was over … if that's what she wanted.

"Hurry up, kid, before the wax drips all over the cake."

"Oh, sorry." I took a breath and then blew out all—both—of the candles.

"So what'd you wish for?" Mac asked as he took a knife and started to cut up the cake.

"If I told you it wouldn't come true."

"Didn't you just say you didn't believe all that stuff?" he asked.

"And didn't you just tell me I had nothing to lose by trying?"

"So I did." He slipped the first piece onto a plate and passed it, and a fork, to me.

I took a little piece and put it in my mouth. "This is really tasty."

"Good to hear. I was a little worried."

"Why would you be worried?"

"Sometimes a cake will turn if it's a few days old," he explained.

"You bought me an old cake?"

"Didn't buy nothing. Donated. And then I remembered your birthday was coming up and I went out and got you some candles. You're sixteen, right?"

"I will be in three days."

"Sixteen is a big one. Got something special planned?"

"My parents are throwing me a surprise party on Saturday."

"Doesn't sound like much of a surprise."

"It isn't, but I won't let them know that I know. I'll act surprised," I said.

"Just family coming?" Mac asked.

"Mainly my friends. That's how I know there's going to be a party. It's hard to keep a secret."

"Nearly impossible," Mac said. "Nice of your parents to try."

"I guess so."

"And that was a nice little donation they made to the Club," he said.

They'd given two thousand dollars. "They can afford it."

"Lots of people *can* afford it. Most just don't give it. I'm grateful. You thank them for me again, okay?"

I nodded my head. He was right, it had been nice of them. They didn't need to do it, but they did.

"You must be looking forward to the party," Mac said.

"I am, but it's going to be different without Berta there," I said. "She's been there for all my birthdays."

"That's right. She's gone down south. Where is it she's from again?"

"Guatemala."

"How long has she been gone for?" Mac asked.

"Almost two weeks. She's going to be gone the whole summer … eight weeks."

"That's a long time to be gone."

"As long as it's only eight weeks, I'm okay."

He gave me a questioning look. "You afraid she won't be coming back?"

I nodded. "I just wonder if once she gets down there she'll ever want to come back." That was the first time I'd actually said those words. Mac was the only person I *could* say them to.

"Is that her saying something, or just you worrying?"

"More me worrying."

"And if she does decide to stay?" he asked.

"Maybe that's where she needs to be right now."

"And will you be okay with that?" he asked.

I didn't know what to say. I knew that she had to go and maybe she needed to stay but I didn't know how I could get along without her and—

"Well?" Mac asked.

I knew what I was saying was right but I still felt like I was close to crying. I took a deep breath.

"I'll be happy for Berta … I'll be okay."

"I don't think," Mac said. "I know you'll be okay." He smiled.

I wanted to believe him.

"So you gonna be getting some presents at your party?" Mac asked.

"A few." One was going to be pretty special. I'd passed everything and there was going to be a car. Funny, I'd starting coming down here to get a car. Now that car was going to help me keep coming down here.

"Here's another present." Mac reached into his pocket and pulled

out his wallet. What was he doing? Was he giving me money or …
He pulled out a small plastic chip and put it on the table.

"Take it."

"Um … thanks," I said as I picked it up.

"Don't thank me. It's not from me. It's from Jack."

"Jack?" I asked in amazement.

"He gave it to my friend to pass on to me to give to you."

"It's … it's really … really nice," I said as I turned it around.

"It is nice. Do you know what it is?" Mac asked.

"Sure. It's a chip."

"It's a two-week chip. It's what you get at the treatment centre when you've been dry for two weeks."

"That's fantastic! I'm so proud!"

"You should be. Jack is doing good … at least he is now."

"Now … what does that mean?"

"The first few days are always the worst. He only hung in for two days before he took off."

I felt my heart drop. "He left?"

"Gone for two days, but he came back."

"Why would he leave?"

"Alcohol's a hard addiction to break. Important thing isn't that he left, but that he came back and has stayed dry for two weeks."

"Two weeks is good … right?" I asked, looking for reassurance.

"Every day sober is good. The longer the better. He might just make it."

"I *know* he'll make it."

"We'll keep our fingers crossed but you gotta remember most people don't make it on the first try, or even the second or the third."

"How many times did it take you?" I asked.

"More than a few," he said.

"But some people do make it the first time, right?"

"Some people beat the odds. I don't know if Jack is going to make it or not. Even he doesn't know that. What I do know is that he wouldn't have had *any* chance without you. Funny, sometimes those long shots work out. Look at you."

"Me?"

"When you first came here I wouldn't have bet a plugged nickel on you even showing your face a second time."

"I guess I surprised you."

"I think you surprised *yourself* even more," Mac said firmly.

I nodded my head. I *had* surprised myself.

"Just remember, we can't control the winning and the losing. All we can control is the caring." He paused. "Enough talking. Let's get ready for the dinner crowd. Get those plates on out there."

I picked up a big stack of plates and started for the dining room. I stopped.

"Mac," I called out and he looked up from the big pot he had started stirring. "Thanks for everything."

"I didn't do nothin'. It was just a cake."

"I'm not talking about the cake."

"I know, but I still didn't do nothin'."

"I couldn't have done it by myself."

Mac smiled. "Who can?" Mac asked. "Who can?"

Do all the good you can, by all the means you can, in all the ways you can, in all the places you can, at all the times you can, to all the people you can, as long as ever you can.

—JOHN WESLEY

In spite of everything I still believe that people are really good at heart.

—ANNE FRANK

Author's Note

I'M OFTEN ASKED where do ideas for novels come from. I know exactly where this story began. I had just finished giving a presentation about Canadian heroes as part of the launch for my book *Run*. A man came up to me to talk about Terry and he mentioned another of his heroes, Roméo Dallaire. He asked if I had ever considered writing a book about Dallaire. I told him I greatly admired the general but didn't know how I could make it into a story. He then told me how to do it. I want to thank Bart Jackson. Without him this book would never have happened. This book is not about General Dallaire, but his experiences in Rwanda, and his incredible book, *Shake Hands with the Devil,* are the inspiration, the foundation on which this book is constructed. I can only hope that by becoming more aware of the tragedies of the past, we are better able to stop them in the future.